LOVE & SK8

NANCY KRULIK

Simon Pulse
New York London Toronto Sydney

1

"Whoa! Check out Buzz!" Zack Landry shouted out, pointing up toward the top of the rickety, wooden, homemade skateboard ramp. At just that moment, Buzz McGrath lifted off from the highest point and flew through the air without touching the ramp. While still in midair, he reached back with his left hand and grabbed the board behind him.

"That was a wicked awesome melloncollie!" Zack said excitedly. "The guy never slips up."

"He's the king," George DiPalma agreed. "He can do anything on that board. I've been working on melloncollies for days and I still slam every time I land." He rubbed the back of his leg, which was sore after one particularly nasty spill.

"There's no one like Buzz," Gina Olsen

1

sighed longingly. She looked over at the pretty, green-eyed girl who was sitting crosslegged on the grass beside her. "He's so hot. Don'tcha think so, Angie?"

Angie Simms shrugged. She didn't think about Buzz much one way or another. *Damn, it's cold.* She zipped the front of her black hoodie and frowned. Angie hated November. It meant winter would be here soon. What a drag. Life in Torren was bad enough without being cooped up inside because of snow. All you needed was one good ice storm, and it would be days before the skaters could use their ramp again. That would leave her with no option but to go home after school on the days she didn't work at the skateboard store. Talk about unbearable.

"It was an okay move," Angie said finally, focusing her gaze on a dead brown leaf that had just fluttered to the ground. "Buzz's done tougher jumps. And he didn't land as smoothly as he usually does."

Buzz strutted over just in time to hear that last bit. His pale gray eyes looked straight into Angie's deep green ones, daring her with the intensity of his stare. "I suppose you could do better, *Van Gogh?*"

Angie frowned. It stunk the way he always made fun of her art. Still, Angie understood why others felt a need to poke fun at her ability to paint and draw. They were jealous—even a little afraid—of the part of her that wasn't at all like them.

To an outsider, Angie wouldn't have appeared any different from anyone else in this group of skateboarding teens. She had straight black hair, which would have been so "Angelina Jolie at the Oscars" had she not dyed the ends bright red. From time to time she would swing her hair back over her shoulders, revealing the six small silver hoops that ran up the edge of each of her ears. And of course there was the jet-black eyeliner that encircled her green eyes, making them seem huge and menacing. No doubt about it, Angie was a skater chick. Maybe the toughest, coolest chick at the ramp. Definitely not someone to be messed with, but a skater chick just the same.

But any outsider who thought that would be wrong. Angie was more than that. A lot more. *She* wasn't going to wind up the way the rest of the skaters would—disgruntled mill-workers in a small Pennsylvania town, just like their parents. Oh sure, for a few years they'd have their skateboarding to give them a distraction from their dull factory jobs. But eventually they'd get too old to make the really tough jumps, and skateboarding would fade away too.

Luckily for her, she had something other than skateboarding to take her mind off the endless monotony that was teenage life in Torren. Her artistic gift was her passion. Her saving grace. *My ticket out of Torren.*

Someday Angie would be a real artist. But not here in Torren, where the locals' idea of art was those old-fashioned Norman Rockwell magazine covers, or paintings of fruit in bowls. No, Angie was determined to be a painter in a big city, where her style of funky, airbrushed graffiti would be appreciated for the amazing gift it was, not treated as a joke by the likes of Buzz McGrath.

"Hey Angie, I'm talkin' to ya!" Buzz barked right in her face. "Do you think you can beat that jump?"

Angie frowned again. She really wanted to pick up her board and storm off, just to let Buzz know he couldn't goof on her art. But he'd given her a direct dare. And there was no way Angie was going to let Buzz McGrath think he'd gotten the better of her.

She stood slowly, stretching her long, muscular legs. Then she flipped her hair behind her, grabbed her custom board, and made her way toward the top of the ramp.

The others watched with genuine approval as Angie flew off the ramp into a perfect ollie. She moved her feet quickly, turning the board beneath her without ever switching her body position. She was totally stoked as she soared through the air. This had to be as close to flying as anything, and Angie loved the feeling.

But even birds have to come down to earth sometime. As the wheels of her board touched down, Angie pumped her fist in the air. *All right! A perfect popshoveit.*

She used her foot to flip up the back of her board, then triumphantly carried it over to where Buzz and the others were sitting. "That's how it's done," she said, shooting Buzz a half smile.

"Not bad," Buzz admitted. "But you've been doing the popshoveit forever. It's time you tried something new. I've got the McTwist down now. I'd be glad to give you a little tutoring so you can get the moves just right."

Zack poked George in the side. "I'll bet he could show her a few moves," he joked.

LeeAnn Macke, Zack's girl, shot him a look. "Get your mind out of the gutter, wouldya, you perv?"

Zack laughed and grabbed her around the waist. "Come on, you know you love it when I talk dirty," he teased, playfully biting her multi-pierced earlobe.

Angie checked the time on a black plastic watch that was barely visible beneath the maze of red and black rubber bracelets encircling her wrist. "Not tonight. I've got to get home," she told Buzz matter-of-factly, pointedly ignoring Zack's comment. "Tomorrow's a school day. And this is senior year. I need decent grades."

Buzz snickered. "For what?"

"Uh, college?" Angie said sarcastically. "I'm going to need at least a partial scholarship if I'm gonna go. And they don't give those to people with lousy grades. I've got a history exam tomorrow, and somehow I don't think the name of the creator of the McTwist is gonna be one of the questions."

"That would be Mike McGill," George noted, giving the name of a famous skateboard champ.

"Gee, you know that and yet you can't get more than a D in history?" Angie sighed. "What *are* those teachers thinking?"

"Mike McGill's more important to me than those stupid European kings Mr. Feldman's always making us memorize. What's that about, anyway? We don't even live in Europe."

"There's more to the world than Torren, Pennsylvania," Angie reminded him.

"Yeah, but we're never gonna see it," Zack moaned. "My old man was born in this place, and he's never been anywhere else—not even Pittsburgh, and that's just a couple of hours away."

"Doesn't mean *we* won't get out of here," Angie suggested.

"Yeah, right," Buzz interrupted. "Now let me get this straight. You're going to be a famous artist, right? Was that in Paris or Rome? No, I think it was New York? L.A.? Chicago?" The others laughed at Buzz's rich-person imitation.

Angie didn't join in with the giggling. Instead, she rolled her eyes. "Go ahead, make fun. But I'm not winding up working in the Morgan Mills making towels like my parents."

"Sure you will," George insisted. "Everyone in Torren works there. Making towels is our entire future. After all, this *is* the Terry Cloth Capitol of the World." He laughed gruffly at the town's official nickname. "Pathetic."

"Not everyone. Not me," Angie insisted.

"No, you won't wind up at the mill," Buzz agreed.

She looked at him, surprised at the sudden show of support.

"You'll be trekking around the country following me," Buzz continued with an air of superiority.

"Excuse me?" Angie asked. She was annoyed with herself for thinking for even a moment that Buzz would be on her side. Buzz never supported anyone but himself.

"Sure. While I'm winning competitions, you'll be sitting in the stands cheering me on. We'll travel the world together. If you're lucky, I'll even let you carry my board on the plane." He held his skateboard out to her playfully. She pushed it away.

"Yeah, but she'll only do that until the baby Buzzes start popping out," Zack joked. "Then it's back to Torren for you, Angie baby. Settle down, raise a family."

Angie sighed. These kids had been her friends for years, and they still didn't know a thing about her. If they did, they'd understand that she wasn't meant to be sitting in someone else's cheering section. And she certainly wasn't going to be the mother of Buzz McGrath's babies. Much as he probably would've wanted it that way.

Buzz had been hot for Angie for forever, although she'd never even so much as kissed him—except for that time in eighth grade when they'd all played spin the bottle in Gina's basement. Since then, he'd been making plays for Angie almost daily. She'd blown him off just as often, but the guy just couldn't get the message.

Not that Buzz had been wasting all his time waiting around for her. Angie was well aware that Buzz McGrath had dated—and probably slept with—at least half the girls in Torren. *The poor half.* The rich girls wouldn't have anything to do with the skaters, or "millbrats," as they called them with disdain. The rich girls had their sights set on the sons of the bankers, lawyers, doctors, and mill owners in town. *Cash on cash.*

In Angie's eyes the rich kids were going to wind up being just as big losers as the millbrats. After all, they'd be stuck in Torren too. Their prisons would be bigger and fancier than the standard track housing the skater kids' families lived in. But they'd be prisons just the same.

"Hey, some of those tournaments have

humongous prizes," George reminded her. "Buzz is gonna be rich. I wouldn't turn down his offer so quickly. Think about it. All that cash, and all you have to do is sit there and cheer him on."

"Yeah, I always thought you were the cheerleader type," Buzz teased.

They all laughed at that—even Angie. She couldn't help herself. The thought of herself—with her overdyed hair, thick black eyeliner, and total screw-you attitude—as a cheerleader was hilarious. She never even wore dresses. There was no way she'd ever get near one of those ridiculous cheerleading skirts.

"Pop that wheel, take that ramp," Zack began to leap around, waving imaginary pompoms wildly like some sort of spastic pep squad leader.

"That's real pretty, Zack," Angie joked as she lifted her bookbag onto her shoulders. "I think the pom-pom girls are having tryouts next week. You should sign up."

"Ooh." Zack smiled lasciviously. "Let me see your pom-poms, girls."

"Forget about it," LeeAnn told him, wrapping a possessive arm around his waist.

"See ya later," Angie said with a laugh as she

slipped one foot on top of her skateboard and started rolling toward home.

"Hey Ange," Buzz shouted as he hurried to catch up with her. "You comin' to the ramp tomorrow?"

Angie turned and shook her head. "Nah. I gotta work."

"What time?"

"I'm going to the shop right after school."

Buzz studied his board for a minute. "I got a little nick in the wood on that last landing," he admitted. "You think you could fix it?"

Angie nodded. Buzz's board had taken a real beating lately, as he'd increased the difficulty of his jumps. He probably could use a whole new deck, but there was no way he could afford it. None of the skaters ever had much cash. Most of them were too busy working on their tricks and jumps to hold down a job for very long.

But in Angie's mind, someone like Buzz, who lived by the board, deserved to have a really awesome design on his deck. She'd fix the chipped wood during her break or something. Besides, Cody, the owner of the Sk8 4Ever skateboard shop where Angie worked part time, usually didn't mind when she helped out kids

11

like Buzz. Cody never tried to make money off the skater kids. He made his living selling fancy custom boards and outfits to wealthy kids who saw skateboarding as a hobby, not a way of life.

"No prob," she agreed. "Just bring your board by the shop tomorrow. I'll smooth down the deck and paint something real sweet over that nick in the wood."

Buzz grinned gratefully. "You're the best, Ange. Really."

"I know it," Angie teased him as she headed down the street. "It's you guys that keep forgetting."

"I never forget," Buzz murmured under his breath as she disappeared from view.

"**W**here've you been?" Angie's father barked at her as soon as she walked in the door.

"Out with my friends," Angie murmured as she threw her bookbag onto the couch and carefully placed her skateboard on the floor of the front closet. She turned toward the kitchen.

"If you're looking for a hot dinner, forget it. We already ate," Mr. Simms informed his daughter. "I told your mother not to hold it for you. If you're not here by six o'clock, that's it. Six o'clock's dinnertime." He leaned back in his chair, picked up the remote, and clicked on the TV. His eyes glazed over slightly as an old seventies sitcom played on the screen.

Angie wasn't the least bit upset by her father's tone. This was not the first time they'd had this conversation—if you could call her father shouting at her a conversation. Charlie Simms was a creature of habit. Up at five thirty, to work at the mill by seven, home at five forty-five, dinner at six. It had been that way every day of Angie's life. Nothing was going to change him now.

"It's okay, I'm just going to grab a sandwich and go up to my room to study." She sniffed curiously at the air. A sweet scent of lavender and spices wafted through the room. "Mmm. What's that smell?"

"Your aunt Dorothy," Angie's dad har-umphed, never taking his eyes from the set. "She's got another of those loony woo-woo types up there." He glanced up at the ceiling, indicating the apartment above the Simms family's garage where Angie's aunt lived.

"Oh hello, dear." Sally Simms, Angie's mom, walked into the living room and handed her husband his after-dinner can of beer. "How was school?"

"Same stuff, different day." Angie shrugged. "I've got a test tomorrow."

"You'll do well," Sally Simms assured her daughter. "You always do."

"I don't know, it's pretty tough this time.

You have to know about all the kings of France."

"Why don't you ask your aunt Dorothy to look into her crystal ball and predict what the questions will be?" Angie's dad chuckled as he popped the top of his beer can. "It'll save you time studying if you already know what the future holds."

Angie shook her head. "In the first place, Aunt Dodo doesn't use her crystal ball. That's just for show. And in the second place, you know she would never use her paranormal abilities to help me on a test. That's cheating."

Angie had always called her Aunt Dorothy "Dodo." When she was little, it was because she couldn't say Dorothy. The name had stuck, a sign of affection between the girl and her aunt.

"You're better off not paying any attention to her phony predictions anyway," Charlie retorted. "It's all a bunch of mumbo-jumbo. I can't believe those rich widows she cons out of cash actually believe what she tells them."

"Aunt Dodo's not a phony. She's helped a lot of people," Angie argued, defending her favorite aunt. Angie hated when her father put down Dodo's psychic skills. The man had absolutely no belief in any kind of psychic phenomenon. He simply couldn't comprehend

15

anything that didn't have a logical explanation. And, of course, there was no logical reason why Aunt Dodo could read the future. She just could. It was a talent, like Angie's art. And it was *very* real. She'd proven it time and time again.

In fact, it was well known in Angie's mother's family that if Sally had heeded her sister's warning, she would never have married Charlie Simms. Dodo had told her sister that marrying Charlie would doom her to an unhappy life. It was all in the tarot cards. Dodo had urged Sally to go away to nursing school and escape the typical mill-town fate.

But Sally had ignored her sister's predictions and advice. Instead she'd gone ahead and married her high school sweetheart. Unfortunately, just as Dodo had predicted, Sally had spent her whole life in Torren, putting up with Charlie's tirades and suffering from his lack of affection and respect. Angie knew there was a part of her mother that always regretted not taking Dodo's predictions more seriously. Angie's dad knew it too—even if he would never admit it.

Rather than argue with the brick wall that was her father, Angie turned her attention toward her mother. "Aunt Dodo's got a customer tonight?"

Sally Simms nodded. "Mmm-hmm. Some rich woman from Eastport, I think. But the session must be almost over. She's been burning incense for about an hour already. According to Dorothy, it enhances your aura and makes it easier to read."

"Oooh, she's reading auras again? Cool. I thought she was just doing tarot cards these days."

"No, I'm pretty sure this is a full reading," Angie's mother replied.

"Will you two shut up?" Charlie demanded, raising the volume on the TV. "I'm watching something here."

Sally Simms slumped slightly and walked toward the kitchen. Angie trudged behind her, taking the time to shoot her father a critical glare.

"So how much more studying do you have to do for the test?" Sally asked as she busied herself making a cold meatloaf sandwich for Angie.

"I just want to read that part about the palace at Versailles one more time."

"Oh, you should talk to Dorothy about that," Sally suggested. "I think she sent me a postcard with that palace on it once. It was beautiful. Like something from a fairy tale."

Angie studied her mother as she prepared a tray. Sally Simms had clearly once been a beautiful woman—you could see it in her high cheekbones and long, thin frame. But life in Torren had certainly taken its toll on her. There were frown lines around her lips and eyes, and she walked with a slight hunch in her shoulders, as if life were just a little too heavy for her to carry around all day.

It was hard for Angie to believe that her mother was even related to Aunt Dodo. Angie's mom played it safe, while Aunt Dodo was a risk-taker who was always searching for the next great adventure. While Sally had been busy working in the mill, her sister Dorothy was backpacking around Europe, earning her keep by reading tarot cards and telling fortunes at festivals at England's Stonehenge or on the streets outside the Prado in Madrid. Dodo was full of stories of exciting men she'd met on trains or in coffeehouses in Paris and Amsterdam. She was a true free spirit, as light and ethereal as Sally was heavy and world-weary.

Which made it all the more curious that she'd returned to Torren. Now *that* was something Angie just couldn't understand. From the time she could walk, Angie had always heard about her aunt Dodo. For years, Aunt Dodo had been a mythical character she'd never met, a relative who sent her cards, letters, and gifts from far-off lands. And then, suddenly, right around Angie's thirteenth birthday, Dodo had appeared, bags in hand, with no explanation. She simply moved into the apartment above the garage and stayed. That had been five years ago, and still Angie was left to wonder why someone like Dodo would decide to return to a place like this.

Angie had tried to ask Aunt Dodo about it once, but she hadn't quite understood her aunt's response.

"I have some unfinished business here," Dodo had replied mysteriously. "And besides, I got tired of running away from what I really wanted."

Was it possible Dodo really wanted to be in Torren?

She certainly *seemed* happy being home. She never had anything less than a beatific smile on her face as she sashayed through the town in her flowing Indian skirts and peasant blouses. No doubt about it, Dodo stood out from the crowd of the usual millrat Torren adults, in their Walmart-issue jeans and polyester shirts. Angie was pretty sure Dodo loved the fact that she looked so different. The way she dressed and acted gave her an air of mystery. It also kept the ordinary people at arm's distance, which was a good thing, since Dodo had no patience for people who were simply ordinary. That was a feeling she and her skateboarding niece shared.

Angie fingered the collection of bracelets on her arm. "Mom, have you and Dad filled out those papers for the Philadelphia Art Institute yet?" she asked, gingerly broaching the subject.

Sally Simms sighed and busied herself cleaning the already sparkling sink. "Not yet, Angie."

"But Mom, you *have* to. If I want to apply for financial aid, they need all the information."

"Well, can't we wait to see if you're accepted before we go to the next step?" Sally asked.

"They want all the paperwork at one time," Angie reminded her mother. "I told you that."

"It's just that your father and I . . . well . . . Philadelphia's a long way from here, Angie."

"Five hours by train," Angie said. "Not so far."

"But you've never been away from home

before. Are you sure you really want to do this? Strange things happen in cities. Can't you work on your painting here?"

Angie could feel rage coming over her. She took a deep breath, trying hard not to scream. "Why would I want to do that?"

Her mother sighed heavily. "Think about it, Angie. You have a good job at that skateboard store. Why would you want to give that up to go off and try to be an *artist*? There's no security in painting or drawing. You're about to graduate from high school. You have to start thinking like a grown-up. And grown-ups have responsibilities."

Angie could feel the angry tears stinging her eyes. How dense could her parents be? Of course she needed to go to school. She needed to be in a place where her talent would be appreciated. *Nurtured.* Someplace where she could grow, change, and take risks. Angie couldn't keep the furor bottled up inside her a moment longer.

"Security?!" she shouted fiercely. "Is that all there is? What does security get you? A job on the loading dock somewhere? Or maybe on the assembly line? And how secure is that? Haven't you heard about the steel mill in Borlingtown?

It's been closed for a year now. All those people on welfare thought they had security too."

"Hey, keep it down in there," Angie's father barked out from the other room. "I'm watchin' somethin'."

"I thought you liked working at Sk8 4Ever," Sally said helplessly, keeping her voice at a near-whisper. She was obviously shocked by the vehemence in her daughter's tone. "You use your art there, painting skateboards."

Angie couldn't really argue that point. As part-time jobs went, hers was a good gig. She spent most of her time at Sk8 4Ever painting her own original designs onto custom-made skateboard decks. But a job like that would only take her so far. Angie's dreams went past the limits of a small piece of wood.

"It's fine, for now," she admitted. "But Mom, I have to get out of here. I'm suffocating in this town!"

"That's ridiculous."

"Why?" Angie demanded. "Does it seem so bizarre that I don't wanna wind up in a dead-end town with a dead-end job and some dead-beat husband? Is it ridiculous that I don't want to turn into you?"

She regretted the words as soon as they left

her mouth. Her mother looked as though she'd been punched in the gut. Her eyes were wide, her mouth was open, and she seemed unable to speak. A wave of guilt washed over Angie. She hadn't meant to hurt her mother. "Mom, I'm sorry. I didn't . . ."

"*Bonsoir* all!" Suddenly Dodo's voice rang out, breaking the pained tension in the room. Sally and Angie looked up at the same time. The expression on their faces was almost identical, filled with overwhelming gratitude that the conversation had been ended by Dodo's arrival.

Angie always loved the sound of her aunt's voice. She sounded so different from everyone else in Torren. Dodo's was a more sophisticated accent, mostly picked up from her years in Europe. It was a mix of British and French, with just a slight touch of slurred *l*'s, a remnant of her Pennsylvania childhood.

Dodo studied Angie's face carefully. "Ah, so you're worried about those college forms again," she suggested.

"You can tell that just by looking at me?" Angie asked her, surprised. "You're amazing, Aunt Dodo."

Her aunt laughed heartily. "Thanks for the

compliment darling, but there's nothing psychic about it. I heard you both arguing. *Mon Dieu,* I think half the people in this county heard you two." She turned to her sister. "What's the big deal? Just fill in the forms."

"I don't see why she needs to go so far away," Sally explained to her sister.

"Oh, *I* understand it," Dodo replied quietly.

"I knew you would," Angie murmured, hugging her aunt tightly. Dodo wrapped her arms around her long, lean niece and held her tight. She looked over Angie's shoulder and tried to make her sister understand.

"She's going to go one way or another," Dodo told her firmly. "You know that. You and I . . . we've been this route before. *Remember?*"

Angie turned around and looked anxiously at her mother. Sally studied the emotion in her daughter's pleading, dark-rimmed eyes. There was a fierce determination there that Angie's mother hadn't seen in years—not since Dorothy had pleaded with their parents to let her go to Boston to participate in a huge study on paranormal activities. Of course Angie's grandparents had said no. The next thing any of them knew, Dorothy was gone—off to Europe for almost twenty years. By the time she'd returned, the girls' parents were both dead and buried. They'd taken the rift between them to their grave, but Dorothy had never regretted being away. She'd never gotten over being angry at them. She probably never would.

That wasn't the way Angie's mother wanted Angie to feel about her. "All right, I'll talk to your dad," she agreed finally, sighing deeply and looking at her sister and her daughter. "I can't fight you both. But Angie, you know I can't guarantee he'll send information about our finances to some strangers all the way in Philadelphia. He's kind of private about things like that. The only thing I can promise is that I'll try and get him to do it."

Angie broke away from her aunt and reached out to hug her mother tightly. "Thank you, Mom," she said, holding her tight.

"Well, I'd love to stay and witness more of this touching scene, but I only came down here to see if I can borrow your car," Dodo said, knowing instinctively that it was time to lighten the mood in the kitchen. "Mine's in the shop again."

"Charlie told you not buy a Japanese car," Sally reminded her sister, seeming happy that for once her husband had been right. "'Buy American,' he told you."

Dodo laughed. "I should listen to Charlie more often," she replied with more than a touch of sarcasm in her voice. "Anyway, can I borrow the car? I need to drive to that big mall over in Harley to pick up some more incense and a new pack of tarot cards. Mine are completely frayed around the edges. Not that I'm complaining. Business has been good these days. People are all worried about whether or not they're gonna lose their jobs. I just wish I didn't have to tell them that their fears are valid."

Angie nodded with understanding. Like any real talent, Dodo's psychic abilities came with responsibility. She couldn't lie to her customers. She could only try and soften the blow of what lay ahead for them.

"I guess you can take the car. Charlie and I aren't going anywhere tonight," Sally said in a melancholy tone. She walked over to the key rack that hung by the back door and removed the car keys. "It's all yours."

"You want to come with me?" Dodo asked her sister.

Sally shook her head. "Charlie hates when I'm not around for family time."

Angie glanced toward the living room,

knowing full well that her father probably wouldn't notice whether or not her mother was home—unless of course he wanted her to fetch him another beer. But she volunteered nothing. She'd said far too much already.

"Thanks Sally," Dodo replied, her voice once again all light and ethereal. "You're the best."

As her aunt turned to leave, Angie silently mouthed an earnest "Thank you."

Dodo gave her a conspiratorial wink, then breezed out the door, her cherry-red and white gauze skirt flowing behind her.

Angie and her mother were left alone in the kitchen once more. They each made a point of avoiding the other's eyes as Sally finished making a sandwich for Angie to take to her room. The argument was over, but the venomous words Angie had spewed were still hanging between them. They'd caused a huge rift in their relationship. It was like the small crack in the blue-and-white flowered plate her mother handed her. The crack hadn't completely broken the plate, but it had left a split that would never be mended.

3

The bells that hung over the threshold of Sk8 4Ever jingled as Angie entered the shop after school the following afternoon. Cody was busy showing some sample decks to a well-dressed mother and her preteen daughter. He looked up for a second and smiled at Angie. Then he went back to demonstrating the importance of buying a maplewood deck as opposed to some of the less expensive premade wood and plexiglass boards that could be purchased in general sporting goods shops.

"It's the strongest wood we have," Cody explained in his strange accent, which was a cross between laid-back Californian and the western Pennsylvania twang the folks in Torren had. "It's rock hard. Seven-ply thick."

The woman looked at him doubtfully. "But

it's so much more expensive than the ones we saw at the department store. We've shopped around quite a bit, you know," she added, letting Cody know that he wasn't dealing with an uneducated customer.

Cody sighed. He'd heard this one before. Ever since big sporting goods companies had entered the skateboarding world, they'd been causing small skateshops like his trouble. The corporations could afford to sell their boards cheaper, mostly because they were mass-produced overseas. But their boards had no character. As far as Cody was concerned, those companies like Nike should've stuck to making sneakers and basketballs.

"Our boards are built to last," Cody told the woman, using his well-rehearsed speech. "They're all handmade, and we use only the best materials. I guarantee everything I do here. You can't say that about those other boards. You wouldn't want the wheels to pop off while she's in the middle of a shoveit or anything, would you?"

The mother opened her eyes wide. "Excuse me?" she asked, insulted.

Angie laughed to herself. She knew what Cody was doing. It was part of a routine he'd devised to grab the attention of a customer who was losing interest. The woman's eyes may have been glazing over as Cody discussed the finer points of maple decks, but his saying "shoveit" immediately brought her back to attention.

"'Shoveit' is a name for a skateboard trick," Angie explained quickly, before the woman became too offended. "It's when you turn the board under your body."

The mother blushed, embarrassed by her obvious lack of knowledge.

"Angie here's quite an artist," Cody said, leaping in before the red-faced woman could scurry out of the store with her tail between her legs. "In fact, she's painted some of our best custom boards." He pointed to the shelf behind him where a few of the decks Angie had decorated with her unique brand of airbrushed graffiti art were on display.

"Oh Mom, look at that one," the woman's daughter squealed, pointing to a lavender skateboard deck that had an airbrushed unicorn and rainbow design on the bottom.

Angie rolled her eyes slightly. That was one of her least favorite designs. No real skater would ever be caught dead with it. Cody had made her paint the pretty picture, knowing full well that unicorns and rainbows were a big draw with eleven-year-old girls—especially those who were just buying skateboards because it was the trendy thing to do.

He should write Avril Lavigne a thank-you note someday for all the business she's brought into the shop, Angie thought ruefully to herself as Cody removed the deck from the display and handed it to the girl.

"Well, I guess my Britty has made up her mind," the girl's mother said with a sigh. She reached into her purse and pulled out a brown leather wallet. "And once she's decided on what she wants, there's no persuading her otherwise."

"Oh thank you, Mom!" Britty leaped up in the air excitedly.

"I'll go in the back and attach the wheels and axles," Cody told the pair.

"You're not going to cover up the unicorn, are you?" Britty pleaded.

Cody smiled kindly at her. "No way. See how there's some blank lavender space here, here, here, and here?" he asked, pointing to different parts of the deck. "Angie's left space for the wheels so it won't ruin the art."

"It's a unique art style you have," Britty's

mother told Angie, with just a little bit of condescension in her voice.

Angie bit her tongue. She'd learned long ago not to discuss her paintings with people who were obviously ignorant. Not that she considered Britty's board one of her finest pieces. "Thank you," she said quietly.

Cody winked at her. Then he turned to the woman and her daughter. "Angie can help you with anything else you might need—pads, wrist guards, a helmet, or maybe some clothes to skateboard in."

"Oh dear, there's so much involved in this," Britty's mother moaned. "I had no idea . . . she can use her bicycle helmet to skateboard in, can't she?"

Helmets. Angie choked back a laugh. Like any of her friends would be caught dead in them. Not that it was smart to skate without a helmet. It was just that they were so uncool.

"Of course she can," Angie told the woman. "But I really think she should wear knee pads and elbow and wrist guards. You definitely take a lot of spills when you're just starting out."

"How long have you been skateboarding?" Britty asked, obviously thrilled to be talking to a real skater chick.

"Since about fourth grade," Angie told her. "You're going to love it."

"Ooh, where'd you get that hooded sweatshirt?" Britty asked, looking longingly at Angie's ever-present, well-worn black hoodie.

"I don't remember," Angie said. "I've had it forever."

"It *is* sort of cute," the older woman agreed tentatively. "I could see Britty in something like that. But definitely not in black. Do you have one in something a little more . . . well . . . a bit . . ."

"We have hoodies in all colors," Angie assured her. She walked around toward the center of the store, where Cody had a complete display of skater clothes. There were some really intense outfits—the kinds professional skateboarders donned for comps—competitions. There was also a kid's section filled with "mom-friendly" versions of street skater clothes like Angie and her friends wore. Angie pulled a lavender terry-cloth hoodie from a hanger. "This one's perfect. It matches your new board."

"Oh, that *is* pretty," Britty's mother said, clearly relieved that even though her daughter was taking up skateboarding, she wasn't going to suddenly become a smaller version of the frightening girl behind the counter, with all those piercings in her ear and red tips in her obviously dyed black hair. She checked the label in the back. "Oh look, this was made at Morgan Mills. Isn't it amazing what they're doing over there these days? It's no wonder Torren is the terry-cloth capital of the world."

Angie bit her lip to keep herself from laughing. "I'll just pack the guards and this hoodie," she volunteered, pulling one of the black and red plastic Sk8 4Ever bags from beneath the counter. "If you wait a few minutes, Cody'll have your board ready."

As Angie ran each item through the scanner by the cash register, the bells above the door to the store jingled once again. She looked up and nodded a hello as Buzz entered the shop.

"Hey Ange," he greeted her.

"I'll be with ya in a sec," Angie replied. "I'm just helping these two finish up. Britty here's buying her first board. She took the lavender unicorn one."

Buzz choked back a laugh. "Cool," he said, trying to sound as sincere as possible—for Angie and Cody's sake. *But that board . . .* they'd laughed about it for days after Cody had made Angie paint it. "You must be really stoked about skateboarding on that one!"

Britty smiled flirtatiously and flipped her shoulder-length blond curls over her shoulder. "I'll bet you're an amazing skateboarder. Do you give lessons?"

Her mother gasped slightly. It was obvious to Angie that she was horrified by the way her daughter seemed to be attracted to this boy. The woman stared pointedly at the large plastic circle in Buzz's left earlobe. It was clearly the largest piercing she'd ever seen. The giant skull emblazoned on his T-shirt didn't exactly thrill her either.

Angie and Buzz met each other's eyes. They'd gotten this reaction from the rich folks in town before. They found the skaters menacing, just one step up from juvenile delinquents.

But Angie wasn't hurt by the disdain in the woman's eyes. In fact, she sort of got a kick out of it. It cracked her up the way rich people judged skaters by how they dressed, never bothering to take the time to find out anything about the person hidden beneath the multiple piercings and thick black rubber bracelets. Of course that was part of the reason Angie dressed the way she did. She wanted to make sure the whole world knew she wasn't a phony like Britty's mother.

Suddenly, Angie felt sort of sorry for the kid. She didn't have a chance. Despite her desperate attempts not to, she was surely going to grow up to be just like her mom. *How pathetic is that?*

"Britty, go sit in the car," the woman ordered her daughter. "I'll wait here for your skateboard."

"But Mom," Britty whined.

"I said *wait in the car,*" her mother repeated through gritted teeth, making an effort not to meet Buzz's eyes as he stared at her with a humorous expression. "Otherwise I'm canceling this whole order right now."

Britty did as she was told. As she left the store, her mother became visibly aware that she was now in the minority. She moved closer to the door, as if ready to leave at a moment's notice if she had to.

"Okay, here ya go," Cody announced as he walked out of the back room with the lavender board in tow. "It's perfect. She'll have a great time with it. There's nothing like skateboarding."

The woman looked at the three of them— Angie, dressed all in black with eyeliner to match; Buzz, whose tight-fitting cap barely covered his stringy brown hair, and whose ragged baggy jeans had slipped low enough to reveal the top of his boxer shorts; and Cody, the aging surfer with a long gray ponytail, thick salt-and-pepper beard, and tie-dyed T-shirt. The thought of her daughter becoming one of them was obviously panicking her.

"I don't even know why I'm buying her all this. She'll be on to something else before I know it," she said, sounding as though she were trying to convince herself that that would indeed be the outcome. "All her hobbies fall by the wayside sooner or later."

Cody shook his head. "Skateboarding's not a hobby. It's a way of life. You oughtta try it. Maybe not freestyle, but you could try slalom. Lots of people your age do that. You just move the board around the cones. You never even have to leave the ground."

The woman appeared shocked at the idea. "No thank you," she said, quickly grabbing her daughter's skateboard from Cody's hands and hurrying out the door.

Angie held her laughter until Britty's mother was safely out of the store. Then she collapsed into an unstoppable fit of giggles. "Did you see her face when you suggested slalom?" she asked Cody.

"That was a good joke, man," Buzz added between guffaws. He laughed so hard he snorted.

"No joke," Cody insisted. "That woman was wound so tight. She needs a little freedom in her life."

"Freedom," Buzz snorted. "Yeah right. Like she's going to find that in Torren."

"Hey man, you make your own prison," Cody disagreed. "And you're the only one with the key to open the cell. You can find freedom anywhere. Me, I always found it on the board, surf or skate. It didn't matter where—I could be on a street ramp, or riding some gnarly waves in Waikiki." Cody glanced at Angie. "But your freedom isn't on the board, is it? You're going to have to look somewhere else."

"Let me guess—at college." Buzz rolled his eyes, unimpressed.

"Maybe," Cody said. "Or just by going someplace where she can paint the way she wants to."

Angie smiled gratefully at Cody.

"Yeah well, she's not the only one with a way out," Buzz insisted gruffly, not letting

Angie be one up on him. "I'm gonna hit the comps circuit as soon as I master a few more kick-butt moves."

Cody glanced up at the shelf of awards above the counter. There were at least fifty of them—huge gold trophies and blue ribbons with medals hanging from them that Cody had won in surfing and skateboarding competitions all over the world.

The kids all knew that Cody had been a champion, probably one of the best ever. What they didn't know was why he didn't skate or surf anymore. He refused to discuss his past.

Angie figured the reason Cody had given up on the comp circuit probably had something to do with the scar on his left cheek. You could barely see it beneath his thick salt-and-pepper beard, but it was definitely the result of a serious injury. Angie didn't dare ask about it. She knew instinctively that it was something Cody didn't want to discuss.

Which didn't mean the kids didn't discuss it among themselves. Speculation about Cody was a regular topic of conversation with them. Ever since he'd just appeared in town five years ago, the stories had been flying about who the stranger really was. Just the fact that he wasn't from Torren made him fodder for the rumor mill. People usually wanted out of Torren, not in.

All of the skaters had their own ideas about what secrets lay in Cody's past. Buzz was positive he'd made some sort of deal with the Mafia and was now part of a witness protection program. Zack figured he'd probably killed someone and was running away from the police. Gina, of course, had a more romantic idea—that Cody had come to this sleepy little town to nurse a broken heart. Angie had a feeling Cody's secret wasn't anything quite as exciting or romantic as the ones her friends had concocted for him. And even if Cody had done something bad in his past, Angie wasn't holding it against him. As far as she was concerned he was a great guy. She wasn't looking any further than that.

"I hope you do it, man. The comp circuit can be a great time," Cody told Buzz sincerely. He turned and looked at the open register. "Angie, be sure to put that credit card receipt with the rest of them, will ya?"

"I can't believe you finally pawned that purple board off on somebody," Buzz congratulated Cody.

"I knew some little girl would love it,"

Cody told him. "Gotta give the public what it wants. It's just good marketing."

"It must kill you to have to deal with people like that, though, dude," Buzz continued.

"Nah," Cody replied with a shrug. "Every dollar just brings me closer to the park."

Ever since Cody'd arrived in Torren five years ago, he'd made no secret of the fact that he thought the town needed a real skatepark—a place with well-constructed ramps where competitions could be held. Maybe not top-draw X-Game comps, but at least some of the smaller ones.

And when there weren't competitions going on, local kids could work on their moves. Cody's goal was to make enough money at Sk8 4Ever to put a down payment on the huge empty lot right near Morgan Mills. Once he had the land, he was pretty sure he could find investors to go in with him on his plans. He planned on hitting up some of his pals from his pro days for the cash.

Cody's dream of building a skatepark in Torren made him a hero to the kids Angie hung out with. Of course, none of them actually believed he could do it—dreams like that just didn't come true in Torren. But just the fact that Cody had a dream—and that it centered on them—set him apart from the rest of the adults they knew.

"Buzz, why're you here, anyway?" Cody asked curiously. "I thought you'd be at the ramp by now."

Buzz shook his head ruefully. "It's my board. I came down too hard, and now I have this nasty delam in the back."

Cody took the well-worn board and studied the nick in the deck. "Ooh, that's a bad one," he agreed. He looked knowingly at Angie. "Let me guess. You were going to fix it for him—for free."

Angie bit her lip. *Busted.*

Cody sighed. "Nothing's free in this world, Buzz."

"But I haven't got any cash . . . ," he answered desperately.

"Who said anything about money?" Cody replied. "All I said is you've gotta pay. There's no way I'm going to let Angie fix this board for nothing. She's my best employee."

"I'm your *only* employee," Angie reminded him.

"And my best," Cody assured her. "Anyhow, it's okay if you want to fix the board. But ol'

Buzz here's gonna have to work off the fee."

"How'm I gonna do that?"

Cody grinned. "You could give that Britty girl a few lessons on her board," he teased. "I'd rent you out at twenty bucks an hour."

Buzz nearly choked. His eyes opened wide with shock. "No way, man," he replied quickly. "I'd rather board with a huge delam on my deck than teach some rich kid how to do an ollie."

"Don't worry," Angie calmed him. "Her momma wouldn't let her within ten feet of you. Did you see her expression when she saw that piercing in your ear?" Angie did a dead-on imitation of the woman's look of fear and disdain.

"Okay, I guess that won't work," Cody agreed, laughing. "So how about you do a little work around here, instead? I just got a huge shipment of grip tape in. You can shelve it for me, and then you can stock the new wheels by size."

"Cool," Buzz agreed.

"Okay," Cody replied, shaking Buzz's hand to seal the deal. He passed the nicked skateboard to Angie. "Now I've got to go to the bank. Angie can show you where everything goes."

As Cody left the shop, Angie turned and

started toward the stockroom. "Come on in the back with me," she told Buzz.

Buzz raised one eyebrow and moved closer to her. He licked his lips like a lion about to capture his prey. "I thought you'd never ask," he told her with more than a hint of flirting in his voice.

Angie rolled her eyes. "Nice try," she said, pushing him away with one hand. "Remember, I'm the one fixing your board. If you don't watch it, I'm liable to paint a pretty purple butterfly over that delam."

Buzz put up his hands and leaped back. Now it was Angie's turn to smile triumphantly. He knew she wasn't kidding. That was just the kind of revenge Angie would enjoy laying on him—spraying a pretty butterfly on his deck. The guys would never let him live that down.

Angie chuckled to herself as a sheepish Buzz followed her into the stockroom. Boys were just so easy. She hadn't met one yet she couldn't control.

4

Angie arrived at Opal's Art Supply just ten minutes before closing on Friday night. There was only one other customer left in the shop by the time Angie arrived—a tall, muscular teenage guy. Probably about eighteen or so, Angie figured. It was easy to see that he was really wealthy—the crest on his prep school polo shirt, his well-ironed chinos, and his hundred-dollar shoes were all a dead giveaway.

Still, Angie had to admit that this kid was a little cuter than most of the preppies—especially the way his longish blond hair kept falling over his eyes. Not that she'd ever consider a rich preppie cute in any *real* way. But it was weird to find a guy like that at Opal's. The prep school crowd didn't usually hang out at art supply stores. Seeing him here sort of piqued her curiosity.

At the moment, an overly solicitious salesman was hovering over the guy, showing him only the finest models of artist's easels. The salesman had barely even bothered to look up when Angie walked into the store. It was obvious he figured her purchase wouldn't bring him the same kind of commission.

"I don't think I need something this elaborate," the guy told the salesman as he examined the thick, glossy, wooden easel the salesman was pointing to. "My mother's just taking up art as a hobby. She wants to paint the flowers in our garden."

Angie laughed slightly. That explained why the guy was here. He was buying a gift for his mother. And Angie knew *exactly* what she must be like: a society woman looking for something to do till she got bored and moved on to another way to pass the time. The kid was wasting his money. He should just buy *Mumsy* a paint-by-numbers kit and call it a day.

Just then, a small round woman with graying hair walked over to her. "Hi, Angie," she said. "I haven't seen you in a while. How's the portfolio going?"

"Okay, I guess, Opal," Angie told the shop

owner. "But I need a new single-action airbrush and a point-three millimeter nozzle."

Opal nodded and led Angie over to an aisle that was filled with all sorts of airbrush accessories. She pulled down two boxes and handed them to Angie to inspect. "Are these what you were looking for?"

Angie studied the text on the boxes just to make sure. She nodded slowly as she approved each object. But when she spotted the price on the bottom of the airbrush, she gasped. "Thirty dollars!" she exclaimed. "That's an awful lot."

"The distributor raised his prices," Opal explained. "I had to raise mine, too."

Angie shook her head with dismay. The nozzle she required for her newest painting was fourteen dollars. She only had thirty-five dollars in her wallet. The nozzle and the airbrush would cost her forty-four dollars. And that was *before* the tax!

"Opal, how about if I pay you thirty-five now and give you the rest next week. I promise as soon as I get paid—"

"Angie, you know I can't do that," Opal said kindly. "We've talked about this before. I know Cody sometimes works that way, but I run a different kind of business."

47

"How about if I give you one of my paintings? Maybe the one of the surfer that you liked so much. That would be a fair barter, don't you think? You always said you thought I was going to be famous some day. Think of it as an investment. . . ." Angie's voice scaled up as she tried desperately to find a way to convince the shopkeeper.

Opal shook her head. "I'd like to help, but I can't pay my rent with paintings." She sighed as she took the boxes from Angie's hands. "You have to pay in full. I'll hold it for you. Just come back when you have the money."

"I have to do this painting now. If I don't finish my portfolio in the next few weeks, I won't have enough slides to send to the art college admissions department. I don't have time to wait another whole week until payday!"

"Can't you borrow the airbrush you use at Sk8 4Ever?" Opal suggested.

Angie shook her head. "It's the wrong type. I need this one." The frustration was becoming too much. Before she could do anything to stop it, Angie began to cry.

At that moment, the salesman who'd been helping the guy with the easels walked over. He whispered something into Opal's ear. Opal looked curiously from the salesman to Angie. Then she nodded and took the airbrush and nozzle and started to hand them to Angie.

"Okay, don't cry," Opal said finally. "I'll tell you what. I'll let you have the nozzle and the airbrush for thirty-five dollars even. You don't even have to give me the painting."

Angie swallowed hard as she struggled to stop crying. "You mean it?" she asked.

"Sure, why not?" Opal asked. "Hey, I'm human. I don't want to stand in the way of you getting into that art school."

Angie eyed Opal carefully. Something in the woman's expression led her to believe that there was more to Opal's change of heart than a sudden desire to help a struggling artist. Slowly she followed the direction of Opal's gaze. It led her straight to the rich preppie kid over by the easels.

He was staring at Angie with a peculiar smile on his face. Obviously he'd been watching the whole scene, and was enjoying it immensely. *Oh man!*

"Hey, why don't you take a picture?" she shouted angrily in his direction. "It'll last longer."

"Angie, please . . . ," Opal warned.

"What?" Angie continued on with the boy, refusing to heed Opal's warning. "You think it's funny that I can't afford this stuff? I'm sorry we can't all be rich enough to buy easels so our moms can paint pretty posies." The words spat out of her mouth like venom. "Some of us have to work for a living. But you wouldn't know anything about that, would you, rich boy?"

The guy turned away from Angie and handed the man a platinum credit card.

"Angie, calm down," Opal said. "I don't want any arguments in my store. Besides, if it weren't for him, you wouldn't be bringing home this airbrush today."

"What?" Angie demanded. "What does he have to do with anything?" She stopped for a moment as it all became clear. "Wait a minute . . . did he . . ."

"I wasn't supposed to say anything . . . ," Opal began.

Angie didn't let her finish. Instead, she stormed over toward the boy. "Look, I don't need your charity," she barked at him angrily. "This is none of your business. I can make it without the help of some rich brat. I don't take anything from anyone."

"You're very welcome," he replied sarcastically as she finished her tirade. "Glad I could help."

Angie stood up tall and tried to look as menacing as possible. Usually that intimidated the rich kids in town. But not this time. The boy stood his ground and matched her stare. A slight smile formed once again on his lips. It was obvious that he found Angie amusing.

"It's not funny!" Angie insisted.

"No one said it is. But I didn't know Halloween was so early this year. . . ."

"What?" Angie asked, glancing at her reflection in the window. "Oh . . ." Long lines of black mascara and eyeliner had trailed down the sides of her face, forming stripes on her cheeks. Her tears had made a huge mess. Quickly, she used the sleeve of her hoodie to wipe away the smeared makeup.

"I didn't really mean anything," he assured her as she cleaned her face. "You just seemed so desperate, and I had my credit card, so . . ."

Desperate! The word felt like a slap in the face.

"Look, it's not that much money," he continued, ignoring the pained look on her face. "A little more than ten bucks, that's all."

"Maybe that's not a lot to *you*!" Angie told him.

"What's the big deal, Angie?" Opal urged. She was anxious both for the sale and to have Angie out of the store before the girl did something stupid. "You said you had to finish the painting. Now you can."

Angie sighed deeply. Opal was right. Angie was backed into a corner—a feeling she despised. She could either take the kid up on his offer or forget about including this piece in her art-school portfolio.

Still, no one said it had to be a gift. "Okay," she said slowly, trying to regain some sense of composure. "But I'll pay you back next week, right after payday. If you just give me your address I can—"

"You don't have to pay me back," the boy said. "Just do something for me in return, okay?"

Angie sighed. She knew there had to be some string attached. "What?" she asked cautiously, unsure of just what a boy like that could possibly want from someone like her.

"When you're famous, remember me as your very first benefactor. I'd like to be known as a patron of the arts."

He walked over to the counter and signed

his credit card receipt, leaving Angie standing there, her mouth slightly open. It was the first time in her whole life someone had done something for her without asking anything in return. She wasn't sure how to take it.

"Have the easel shipped to my address, will you?" the wealthy teen told the salesman who'd been helping him. He resisted the urge to flash a triumphant smile in Angie's direction, but she could see it forming on his lips just the same.

Which only served to make her angry once again.

"Certainly," the salesman said. "And thank you."

Opal sighed with relief as the boy left the shop, ending the incident. The last thing she needed was a problem with Carter Morgan III, grandson of the most powerful man in four counties and heir to the Morgan Mill. Angie must not have known who he was, otherwise she never would have messed with him.

The shopkeeper packed the airbrush and nozzle into a plastic bag and handed it to Angie. "That wasn't exactly gracious of you. He was just trying to do you a favor."

"He was *pitying* me," Angie insisted. "I don't need favors like that."

"You've got a real chip on your shoulder, you know that?"

"It's guys like him who put it there." Angie tucked the art supplies into her backpack. "At least I'll never have to see him again."

"You can never be sure," Opal remarked.

"Somehow I don't think we'll be crossing paths in the near future," Angie said confidently as she walked toward the door.

"Need a lift?"

Angie looked up as she heard the sound of his voice. She couldn't believe her ears. Was this boy completely dense? What could she possibly have said in there that would've made him think she'd take a ride from him? And yet, there he was, right outside of Opal's, standing next to his little silver custom Volkswagen Beetle convertible.

"No thanks, I'll walk," Angie said gruffly. She turned and started down the street.

"I don't mind, really," Carter said. "I owe you at least that much."

"You owe *me*?" Angie stopped and turned around.

"Sure. I really upset you. And I feel bad about it," he replied, sounding incredibly sincere.

"Don't feel bad. Just go away."

Carter shook his head in amazement. "You're really something, you know that?" He shot her an appreciative grin. "The girls I know love it when guys buy them things. The more expensive the better. Hell, they *expect* it. But you . . ."

"I'm nothing like the girls you know," Angie scoffed.

"No you're not," he agreed. "But I'd like to *get* to know you."

"Why're you so interested in me?" she asked him.

"Let's just say I have a thing for girls who reject my gifts," he teased, flashing a sly, sexy grin. The effect was not lost on Angie. "Come on, hop in. I'll even put the top down. That way you won't have to endure my prep school odor."

"Your *what*?"

The boy laughed. "You think I'm not aware of what you and your friends say about us? That you could smell preppies a mile away?"

"How'd you know . . . ?"

"I know a lot more than you think," he continued smugly. "I know that you and your skater buddies hang out at the loading dock behind Morgan Mill drinking beer and goofing on kids like me. Which, incidentally, isn't exactly fair, since you've never once tried to talk to one of us."

"We never try to talk to *you*? How about you and *your* friends? You cross the street when you see one of us coming toward you on the sidewalk. We see the fear and disgust on your faces when you run into a group of us hanging out in the park or at the mall."

"I think you enjoy that," Carter answered calmly, a knowing look coming over his slate-blue eyes. "But I can't imagine why."

That infuriated Angie. This kid acted like he knew everything about her—when he didn't really know a thing. She wanted to hit him. She wanted to wipe that smug grin right off his face. Angrily, she took the bag with the airbrush in it and hurled it onto the hood of his car.

"Whoa! What's that about?" he demanded. "What'd my car ever do to you?" He pointed to the dent in the hood that she had caused. "I'm going to have to have that fixed, you know. How about your new gift? Do I have to replace that, too?"

Angie turned beet red. *Oh man.* She was in trouble now. "I'm—I'm sorry," she stammered. "I didn't mean to . . . I'll . . . I'll pay you back, whatever it costs." Angie looked into Opal's bag. "I think the airbrush is okay. It's all boxed up. . . ."

"Relax," he said. "It's just a dent. No big deal." He stopped and smiled playfully at her. "But I do think you need to get to the root of this deep-seated anger you have against small cars."

Angie laughed despite herself.

"That's better." He gave her a wink. "So whaddaya say we discuss this problem of yours over dinner?"

Angie stared at him, amazed. After all this, he wanted to take her out? Obviously this kid wasn't used to anyone saying no to him. In fact, maybe he was interested in her because she was totally *un*interested in him. So, naturally, Angie did the one thing she was certain would turn him off. She said yes.

"Okay, I give in. Tomorrow night, eight o'clock."

"Great!" Carter exclaimed excitedly. He pulled a Palm Pilot from his pocket. "Just give me your address. I'll pick you up and we can go—"

"That won't be necessary," Angie rolled her eyes and gently placed her hand over the screen.

She smiled coyly. "Just meet me at Hamburger Heaven at eight o'clock."

He studied her face for a moment, unsure of what to make of her choice of restaurants. "Hamburger Heaven, huh?" he murmured, mulling over the idea. He sighed. "Okay, it's a date."

"See ya there," Angie replied as he jumped into his car and closed the door. She smiled to herself as he drove off. She knew she'd seen the last of that jerk. There was no way he'd ever show up at Hamburger Heaven. A kid like him wouldn't have the guts.

"We missed ya at the ramp, Angie," George said, taking a sip of his orange soda. It was Saturday evening, the day after Angie's incident at Opal's. "You shoulda seen Buzz. He was totally on. He did a perfect three-sixty flip without even breaking a sweat!"

Buzz smirked triumphantly in Angie's direction. "It was no big deal."

"It was too," George insisted. "It was pure genius, dude."

"Sorry I missed it," Angie told him sincerely. "But I was painting all morning, and then I had to work." She leaned back on the bench and sighed. Another Saturday night at Hamburger Heaven. They were definitely in a rut.

"What were you painting?" LeeAnn asked,

sounding only vaguely interested. She swiped a fry from Zack's plate.

"Well, I—," Angie began.

"Hey!" Zack shouted. "That's mine."

"Come and get it," LeeAnn teased, placing the tip of French fry in her mouth while letting the rest dangle.

Zack bit the end of the fry and kept nibbling until his lips reached LeeAnn's. "Mmm," he joked. "I don't know which I like better, french fries or French kisses."

"You'd better know which . . . ," LeeAnn joked, playfully hitting him over the head.

"It's you, babe, always *you*," Zack vowed, leaning over and shoving his tongue into her mouth.

"Hey, get a room you two," George groused.

"As I was saying," Angie continued in a playfully stern voice, "I painted a picture of the palace in Versailles. You know, the one we learned about in history."

The others looked at her blankly.

"Forget it," Angie sighed. "Anyway, it was really tough and intricate. I was glad I had a new nozzle to work with."

"So you saved up enough for the stuff?" Gina asked.

Angie shook her head. "Not exactly. Almost, though."

"Then how'd you get it?" Gina continued.

"Did you lift it?" LeeAnn asked excitedly.

"No!" Angie insisted. "I wouldn't do that. Actually, it was the weirdest thing. I couldn't afford the nozzle *and* the airbrush, but some rich preppie offered to pay the difference."

Up until that moment, Buzz had been busy looking out the window and eyeing a bleached blonde who was straddling the back of her boyfriend's Harley. But now his attention was completely on Angie.

"What preppie?" he asked her.

"I don't know. He didn't give me his name."

"What'd he want in return?" Buzz demanded.

"Nothing," Angie told him. "That was the weird part."

"Oh come on, they all want something. Rich guys don't do anything for nothing," Buzz insisted.

"This one did."

"I don't believe you," Buzz said. He looked at her accusingly.

"Come on, not all guys are like you," Angie told him.

"They just wish they were," Zack joked.

He gave Buzz a congratulatory pat on the back, and pointed to where the blonde was sitting. Now she was obviously eyeing Buzz. "My man!"

But Buzz had lost interest in the biker chick. He was focused on Angie. "What were you doing, hanging with that guy?" he demanded.

"What, are you nuts?" Angie answered. She was insulted. "Nothing. I needed an airbrush, he felt like being generous. He didn't want anything from me, I swear. Besides, I don't know what the big deal is. It's not like I'm ever gonna see him again."

"Was he cute?" Gina asked.

Angie shrugged. "He looked like the rest of them. They all come from the same cookie cutter."

"Let me guess," Buzz snapped. "He was about six feet tall with straight blond hair."

"How'd you know that?" Angie asked, surprised.

"'Cause he's standing right out there," Buzz replied, pointing to the edge of the parking lot.

Angie whipped around quickly. Sure enough, there he was, standing next to his silver Volkswagen. "I never thought he'd have the guts . . . ," she murmured under her breath.

"The guts to do what?" Buzz demanded.

"Well, he said he wanted to take me out to eat," Angie explained, incredulous. "I told him to meet me here. But I really couldn't imagine a kid like him coming to a place like this."

"Well, he did," Buzz said, sounding very much like a jealous boyfriend. "Now get rid of him."

The proprietary tone in Buzz's voice really pissed Angie off. He'd no right to tell her what to do. She didn't belong to him—or to anyone else for that matter. She certainly wasn't about to do anything just because Buzz ordered her to. Angie jumped up from the table.

"Watch it," Buzz hissed at her.

"Watch *this*," Angie told him as she strutted out of the restaurant, smiling triumphantly.

"You said eight, right?" Carter said. Angie took his arm in hers, making sure they were in plain view of the others. He seemed surprised at her sudden show of affection, but said nothing.

"Mm-hmm," Angie murmured.

"Sorry I'm a little late. I didn't—"

"Let me guess, you don't know this side of Torren real well," Angie interrupted him.

"Actually I was going to say that I didn't

have gas, and I had to drive around till I found a station that was open," he replied.

"Oh."

Carter smiled slightly, pleased that he'd thrown her off guard. "Are you hungry?" he asked her.

Angie nodded. "I'm always hungry. They make the best cheeseburgers here."

"Now that's what I like to hear," Carter laughed. "Most of the girls I know eat nothing but salad with lemon when they're out. I'm so sick of hearing about diets."

"I don't diet," Angie assured him.

Carter looked her over appreciatively. "You don't need to."

"I skateboard a lot. Makes me hungry."

"Well then, let's go in," Carter said. "I want to try one of those cheeseburgers you recommended."

"You might want to go for a chili burger," Angie suggested. "Except, they're kind of spicy."

"I like things spicy," Carter assured her as they walked into Hamburger Heaven. He stopped in front of the cash register. "Do we have to wait to be seated, or . . ."

"No." Angie started laughing. "There's no hostess here. You just grab a booth anywhere."

She plopped down in one near the door. She laughed again as she watched the expression on Carter's face as he looked at the seat on his side of the table. The plastic was torn and a few springs were popping through. Still, Angie had to give him props for sitting down without complaint.

She wasn't nearly as pleased with the behavior of her friends, however. They raced over and grabbed the booth right behind Angie and Carter's. Buzz positioned himself in the seat that faced Angie. She made a point of looking directly at Carter and avoiding Buzz's glare.

"So, what'll ya have?" the waitress asked as she walked over to the table, pad in hand.

"Do you have any menus?" Carter asked her politely.

The waitress heaved a heavy sigh. "Where do ya think ya are?" she asked him, pointing to a blackboard over the counter. "It's all there."

"I'll have a chili burger and a vanilla shake," Angie told the waitress.

"Sounds good," Carter said. "I'll have a chili burger too. Make mine medium rare."

The waitress laughed. "Oh sure, medium rare. Just a little pink in the center." She walked off, still chuckling at that one.

"Did I say something funny?" Carter asked Angie.

Angie shook her head. "No. It's just that all the burgers are cooked pretty much the same here."

"Oh."

They fell into silence, each a little uncomfortable with the situation.

Just then, George peeked over the side of his booth. "Ya got any cash, Ange?" he called over to her. "We're trying to get enough to get a basket of cheese fries."

"Maybe her date has a buck or two," Buzz suggested with a snide air. "He looks like his wallet's full."

"Actually, I . . ." Carter started to reach for his wallet, but Angie reached across the table and rested her hand on his arm.

"Don't bother," she said. "I got it." She reached into her front pocket and pulled out a wrinkled dollar bill. "You owe me," she told George.

"So, did you hear what's going on at that empty lot by the mill?" Angie overheard Buzz ask the others. "The one Cody's saving up for? The town council's being a real pain about it. They don't want to give him permission to buy it for a skatepark. They said it's something about zoning or some other crap."

"That's what they say. But you know it's all about that aging asshole Carter Morgan," Zack added. "He doesn't want a skateboard park next to his mill. Heck, he doesn't want a skateboard park anywhere! And those wusses on the council are all on his payroll. They'll do whatever he says."

"I don't know what Old Man Morgan's problem is," LeeAnn said. "What does he care if we skate? It's not like we're going to bother him."

"You know how *rich people* are," Buzz said, emphasizing the words and speaking loudly for Angie's sake. "They want to control everyone. And if they can't control you, they want to get rid of you. They'd be just as happy if we all dropped dead."

"Old Man Morgan's almost dead," George mused. "Wouldn't it be funny if they buried him in the empty lot and we built the skatepark over him? It'd be like skating on his grave." He collapsed in a fit of laughter at the thought of it.

Angie rolled her eyes. Usually, she'd be right in there, goofing on rich kids with the others. But for some reason, tonight she was slightly embarrassed by their behavior. It was a weird feeling. Like she was on the outside looking in—at her own crowd.

"You know, I don't even know your name," she said, trying to bring fresh conversation to the table. "I'm Angie Simms."

"And I'm . . ." Carter stopped for a moment. Angie saw him squirming in his seat. Buzz and his crew must be really making him uncomfortable. "I'm Chad Montgomery," he said quietly.

"Chad, huh?" Angie said. She studied his face. "You look like a Chad," she said finally.

Carter couldn't meet her eyes. "I do?" he asked her. "You're the first person to ever think so."

"Well, I mean, Chad must be a very popular name with your crowd," Angie said. "It sounds so . . . so . . ."

"So preppie," Carter suggested.

"Well, I guess so." Angie blushed slightly under his stare. She was relieved when the waitress appeared with their burgers.

"Two chili burgers," the waitress said, placing the giant, sloppy sandwiches in front of them. She looked at Carter and laughed. "I hope it's just the way you like it."

"I'm sure it'll be great," Carter replied. He placed a napkin on his lap and reached for his knife and fork. But he stopped as he saw Angie pick up her chili burger and take a huge bite.

"Mmm . . . this is as good as it gets," Angie said as tomato sauce dripped down her chin. Carter picked up his napkin and reached across the table, gently wiping the sauce from her face. That act, so simple, yet so intimate, took her by complete surprise. "Um, thanks," she murmured.

Carter smiled at her as he took a bite of his own burger. "Whoops," he said, laughing as a big stream of chili slipped off the bun and onto the table. "Boy, this is tough to eat," he said.

"It takes practice," Angie giggled.

"I guess," Carter agreed. He picked up the burger again, but this time his watch slipped off his wrist, and landed with a clank right in the puddle of tomato chili he'd just dropped. The tomato sauce spattered a bit, leaving tiny orange droplets on the front of his shirt. "Darn clasp," Carter moaned as he picked up the shiny gold watch, wiped it clean with a napkin, and put it back on his wrist.

"You want to get some soda water or something for that shirt?" Angie asked him.

Carter shook his head. "Nah. That's why they invented washing machines," he replied in a relaxed manner. "So tell me about your painting. What kind of stuff do you do? Is it some sort of abstract airbrushing? Or is it like pop art?"

Angie looked at him, surprised. No one in Torren ever seemed particularly interested in her artwork, other than her Aunt Dodo. She'd never had to put a label on her work, and now she wasn't quite sure how to answer him. "Well, I do most of my painting with an airbrush," she said slowly, trying to come up with the words to describe the paintings she'd been working on most recently. "It's not really abstract, it's more of a modern, kind of graffiti-esque look, but I guess it has some impressionism in it too, because sometimes I paint things the way I feel them."

"So you're kind of a modern-day Monet," Carter mused.

Angie was impressed. None of her friends even knew what an impressionist painter was— never mind being able to name one. "Well, that's a bit of a stretch," she replied modestly. "But I guess the sentiment is the same."

"Monet was kind of a radical in his time,

like you," Carter suggested. "I think that's part of why I love his work. I'm a fan of Manet, too. And of course, Van Gogh. But I think Pissaro is my favorite of all."

"How do you know so much about art?"

Carter took a huge sip of his shake. "I spent a lot of time at the Musee D'Orsay when I was in Paris last summer. If you love impressionist art, you'd go crazy there."

Angie listened carefully as he passionately described the art he'd seen in Paris, telling her about his visit to the Picasso Museum and, of course, the Louvre. She'd only seen the artists' works in books, or on postcards her aunt Dodo had in her scrapbooks. But he'd seen them real and up close, and he was able to describe them in magical detail. Angie found herself forgetting that he was some rich preppie that she was supposed to hate. Instead, she reveled in the opportunity to discuss something so important to her.

"So, do you want to be an artist?" she asked him finally.

"Me? No way," Carter exclaimed. "I'm strictly an afficionado."

"The world needs more of those." Angie smiled shyly. "You know, I never really thanked you for bailing me out at Opal's the other day."

"Yeah, you did," Carter assured her. "You agreed to join me for dinner at this lovely restaurant." He glanced over to the griddle, where a short-order cook in a grease-stained apron was flipping burgers.

"I guess this isn't exactly what you're used to, but—," Angie began.

"You never expected me to show up, did you?" Carter interrupted her. He looked her straight in the eye, watching for her reaction.

"Sure, I . . ." Angie stopped herself mid-sentence. There was no denying it. Besides, she was a terrible liar. "I guess not."

"It's okay. I came on pretty strong," he admitted. "You were right to try and get rid of me. But as you can see, it didn't work. I'm here."

"You decided to bravely go where no preppie had gone before," Angie giggled, paraphrasing the old *Star Trek* line. She took one last loud slurp from her frappé glass, scarfing up a bit of vanilla shake.

"You two finished?" the waitress mumbled as she came over to the table and reached for their empty food plates.

"Do you want anything else?" Carter asked Angie.

Angie shook her head. "I'm full."

"I guess we'll have the check, please," Carter told the waitress.

She nodded and pulled the pencil from behind her ear. "I'm just warning you. We don't take no credit cards."

"That's okay," Carter assured her. "I've got cash."

"I'll bet you do," the waitress murmured as she handed him the bill for the meal. "That'll be thirteen-fifty."

Carter pulled a crisp twenty-dollar bill from his wallet and handed it to her. "Keep the change," he added gallantly.

Angie shook her head slightly and frowned. She'd almost started to like this guy, until he started flashing his cash around. Like that was going to impress her or something.

"What's the matter?' Carter asked, noticing the sudden change in expression on her face.

"Nothin'," Angie muttered.

"No, something's bothering you. What'd I do?"

"Do you think throwing your money around makes you better than us?" she demanded.

"What do you mean?" Carter was genuinely confused.

"The bill was thirteen-fifty," Angie told him. "So what's with the twenty?"

"I gave her a good tip. She works hard."

"Yeah, how would you know?"

Carter sighed. "I know because I worked as a busboy last summer at my parents' club. Working in a restaurant is tough."

Angie snorted. "You were a busboy in a restaurant. Yeah, right!"

"I was," he insisted. "I really wanted a motorcycle, but my parents refused to let me get one. So I went out and earned the money for it."

Angie wasn't sure which shocked her more—the fact that he'd worked as a busboy or that he rode a motorcycle. Neither one fit her idea of a rich kid. "You have a *bike*?"

Carter nodded. "A real sweet Honda. It's not big or anything, but it has a smooth ride."

"So how come you came here in your car?"

"I didn't want you to get the wrong impression," Carter joked. "I'm not a tough biker guy."

Angie looked at his clean, neat jeans, Abercrombie shirt, and expensive leather boots. "No kidding," she teased.

Carter laughed with her—a rich, genuine chuckle, free of any of the anger or hostility her friends often had lurking behind their laughter. She liked the sound of it.

This is so weird. It's like some sort of boy-meets-girl eighties movie, Angie thought to herself. She stared across the table into the slate-blue eyes of this perfect stranger with whom she'd obviously made a real connection. She and Carter were from different worlds, and yet here they were, having a great conversation, laughing, eating . . . *on a date.* Angie suddenly realized she'd never been on a real date before—one where she and the guy sat alone, and he picked up the tab at the end of the meal. The skater kids always hung out in a pack, and whoever had the most money at the end of the night was stuck with the tab. Since Angie was the only one with a job, more often than not *she* was that person.

Angie sensed that she wasn't the only one who felt the connection between the two of them. He felt it too. She knew that for sure when suddenly, without warning, he leaned across the table and kissed Angie gently on the lips. Then he leaped backward in his seat, as though even he was surprised by what he'd done.

"What the . . . ," Angie stammered.

"Oh, wow. I'm sorry," Carter apologized. "I didn't mean to . . . it just sort of seemed like . . . oh wow. Hey Angie, I . . ."

"It's okay," Angie told him softly. "I kinda liked it."

Carter seemed surprised. "You did?"

Angie nodded. "I kinda like you, too." And to show him how much, she leaned across the table and returned the kiss.

The skaters had long since left the booth in the restaurant. Their cash had run out quickly, and so had their interest in what was going on in Angie and Carter's conversation. But even though they'd moved the party into the parking lot, Buzz had never lost sight of Angie. And although she didn't know it, Buzz had seen her kiss the preppie . . . *the enemy.*

"Hey you guys, check out this car," Buzz shouted, racing over toward Carter's silver Beetle at the edge of the parking lot. "I say let's bounce it!"

"Whoo hoo!" Zack shouted in agreement. He rushed over to Buzz's side with George right behind him. Together, they began pushing on the hood of the car, bouncing it up and down and moving it around the parking lot.

Bang. The side of the car crashed into the truck beside it. "Oh look," Buzz said with fake concern. "He got a dent. Now the car's lopsided. Whatever shall we do?"

"We could do the other side," Zack suggested excitedly, pressing harder on the hood of the car.

"Oh yeah!" George agreed, giving the hood a hard push.

By now, a crowd had gathered around Buzz, Zack, and George. The other Hamburger Heaven customers were cheering them on with the kind of vigor that could only be achieved through a mixture of boredom and beer.

"Oh man, my car!" Carter shouted. He raced out of the restaurant, leaving a shocked Angie standing there on her own. Quickly, she hurried off after him.

"Chad, be care—," she started. But her voice was drowned out by the noise in the parking lot.

"Get off of my car!" Carter demanded.

Buzz plopped himself down on the hood of the car, hard. He folded his arms across his chest. "I don't think so."

"I said get off," Carter insisted again.

"Sorry dude, I don't talk prep. Do you, Zack?"

Zack shook his head as he leaped up onto the hood of the car beside Buzz.

Carter shook his head and pulled the keys from his pocket. He opened the door and hopped in.

"Chad, are you crazy?" Angie asked.

At first, Carter looked at her oddly. Then he slammed the door shut. "Sorry Angie, I hate to eat and run, but I think it's time for me to go." He winked in her direction. "Next time I pick the restaurant, okay?"

Before Angie could answer, Carter revved up the engine.

"He wouldn't dare," Buzz laughed, staying put atop the car.

But Buzz underestimated Carter's anger. Carter popped the Bug into drive, then quickly hit the brake. Buzz and Zack flew off the hood and landed in the parking lot. Before they could get up and chase him, Carter had whipped the Beetle around. He sped off out of the parking lot, leaving Angie standing alone in the night.

LeeAnn leaned on the counter by the cash register at Sk8 4Ever and stared at Angie through tired eyes. It was Sunday morning, and LeeAnn and Zack had been up all night. Sure, some of it had been fun, but most of the night they'd been arguing about Angie.

"Oh man, the guys are really pissed at you, Ange," LeeAnn informed her. "What were you thinking, anyway?"

"I never figured he'd show up," Angie told her. "I assumed he'd be too scared." Her mind raced back to the parking lot the night before. "Maybe he should've been."

"Oh come on. They were just having a little fun," LeeAnn defended her friends. "Besides, the dents are small."

"Yeah, but he's still gotta pay to fix them,"

Angie reminded her. "I don't know what they were thinking."

"What're you defending the preppie for?" LeeAnn began.

"His name is Chad," Angie reminded her.

"Oh right. Ch-a-a-d," LeeAnn's voice took on a singsongy quality as she said the name. "Anyway, what're you worried about him for? Did you see what he did to Zack and Buzz? Those guys could have been seriously hurt."

Angie nodded. She knew what LeeAnn meant. It wasn't cool the way Chad had gone after Buzz and Zack.

Angie knew that it would be best to forget about everything that had happened last night. After all, Chad might've seemed really sweet and smart and all that, but he was still from the other side of the tracks. And there was no way anything could ever come out of it. She was a skater, and he was a preppie. Some lines were too hard to cross.

She reached down below the counter and picked up a freshly painted black deck and a piece of white chalk. As LeeAnn watched over her shoulder, Angie began to sketch a design onto the wood. Her hand moved easily across the board, leaving light, quick chalk marks. She seemed almost unaware that LeeAnn was still in the store. She was lost in some sort of artistic trance that very few people ever experienced or understood.

At first the marks seemed to have no rhyme or reason, but then a pattern began to emerge.

"Hey, that's a cool one!" LeeAnn exclaimed as she recognized the drawing as a skeleton on a skateboard leaping over a bottle of poison. "Who's that for?"

"No one special." Angie shrugged. "It's just a board for the display. It'd have to be for a real skater, though. No rich brat's mom's gonna buy this one." She smiled. It felt good to know that someone who was really dedicated to skating would be ollieing on one of her boards. It was frustrating watching so many of her pieces of art going to kids like that Britty girl who'd been at the store.

"Did you finish *your* new board yet?" LeeAnn asked her.

"Almost," Angie replied. "Cody's been really cool about letting me use his paints and stuff after hours. You wanna see it?"

LeeAnn nodded excitedly. "You're the only one of us who's had a new board in ages."

"I'm the only one of us who can *afford* it,"

Angie reminded her. "It wouldn't kill you to get a job, you know."

"Hey, there's only one skate shop in town," LeeAnn reminded her. "And you already work here. Where am I supposed to get a job? Think about it. Do you think the Clothes Closet's gonna hire me?"

The thought of LeeAnn working in a place like the Clothes Closet was hysterical. That place was so uptight—it sold nothing but discount versions of the kinds of fashions girls read about in teen magazines. At the moment, LeeAnn was wearing a pair of oversized black flares that hung down far lower than they should have on her hips, and a tight black Linkin Park T-shirt. A thin silver chain swung along her left cheek, connecting the small stud in her nose to a similar post in her ear. Her nails were painted black, the same color as the heavy eyeliner that accented her soft brown eyes. Angie had to laugh. The only teen magazine that might feature LeeAnn's current outfit would be *American Goth*.

"So let's see the board," LeeAnn urged.

"It's in the back," Angie told her. "I'll go get it."

LeeAnn waited in the front of the store

while Angie headed into the storeroom. The minute Angie was out of the room, the door to the shop opened, and the jingling bells signaled Buzz and George's arrival.

"Where is she?" Buzz demanded of LeeAnn.

"In the back," LeeAnn said quietly. "Hey Buzz, lay off her. It wasn't her fault last night. She never thought the guy would show up."

"Yeah well, she didn't seem too anxious to see him go," Buzz shot back. "Someone's got to remind her who she is."

"And you're that person?" LeeAnn asked.

"Who'd be better?" George questioned her. "You? You and Gina probably thought that jerk was hot or something."

"Oh, yeah, right," LeeAnn scoffed. "Preppies are my fantasy men. It's all I think about when I'm making out with Zack."

"Bet Zack would love to hear that one," George chuckled.

"Angie's got no interest in rich kids," LeeAnn assured him. "She knows where she comes from."

"Yeah, and I'm pretty sure of where I'm going," Angie interrupted as she walked out of the stockroom. "And that's out of this stinkin' town."

LeeAnn blushed. "I'm sorry, Ange. I was just trying to . . ."

"I know what you were trying to do," Angie assured her kindly. "But you don't need to fight my battles with Buzz or anyone else. I can do it all on my own."

"I don't want to fight you, Angie," Buzz told her, his pale gray eyes taking on a certain menacing look. "I'm just warning you, stay away from that guy. He's trouble."

"I can take care of myself," Angie answered him.

"It didn't look that way to me last night," Buzz shot back.

"Who told you to look?"

Buzz's face grew red. He wasn't used to people standing up to him. In fact, Angie was pretty much the only one in their crowd who did.

"Hey, is that the new board?" LeeAnn asked, changing the subject before things got any worse.

"Mm-hmm. It's all finished." She held out the board for them to see.

"Wow, that's so cool!" George exclaimed, studying the brightly colored, interlocking, roughly drawn squares and rectangles that

Angie had airbrushed onto the bottom of the deck of her new board. "There's no other board like that in this county."

"There's no other board like that any-where!" LeeAnn exclaimed. "It's gorgeous. I think it's too beautiful to ride. That should be hanging in a museum somewhere."

"Actually, it's based on a work called *The Snail* by Henri Matisse," Angie said. "I saw it in one of my aunt Dodo's art books."

"Dodo." George guffawed. "Perfect name for her."

"Torren's own psychic hotline," Buzz added with a snort.

Angie shot them both an angry look. She couldn't bear it when anyone made fun of her aunt. Especially not those two. Her aunt Dodo had more class and intelligence in her little finger than Buzz and George did in their whole bodies.

But there had been enough bad blood between Angie and the other skaters lately. No point making things worse. She turned toward LeeAnn. "Matisse's painting was made of gouache on cut and pasted paper, but I tried to do something similar, in my own style. I think it worked out okay."

Angie looked at LeeAnn. Her friend's eyes had glazed over. She had absolutely no idea what Angie was talking about. For a moment, Angie wished she could talk about her new board with Chad. Surely he'd know who Matisse was. He'd probably seen some of his paintings up close.

Buzz took the board from Angie's hands and studied the bend in the wood. "Killer concave!" he exclaimed, obviously impressed. "This is a wicked deck, Angie."

On the other hand, Chad wouldn't have caught that detail. The rich kids never thought about the actual construction of the board, or why it was so important that the wood of the deck be curved in just the right way. That was something only Buzz and the rest of the skaters got.

"Wait till Zack sees it," Buzz continued. "He's gonna freak."

Angie smiled proudly. It took a lot to impress Buzz, but her board had done it.

"You gotta try this thing out," George said, rolling one of the new wheels around with his fingers. "Are you coming to the ramp today?"

"As soon as I get off work here," Angie assured him. "Probably around five."

Buzz looked at her skeptically. "What, no

plans with your rich lover boy?" he asked sarcastically. "Isn't he flying you off to Europe on his yacht?"

Angie rolled her eyes. "A yacht is a *boat,* you moron." She laughed as Buzz blushed a deep red. "Anyway, I don't think I'll see him anymore. He doesn't have my phone number or my address. And I'm pretty sure you guys have scared him away from Hamburger Heaven forever."

"That was the idea," Buzz told her pointedly.

"Yeah, well, it worked," Angie replied, avoiding Buzz's triumphant grin. "Anyway, you guys better get out of here. I've got work to do. I'll meet you at the ramp, I promise."

The bells to the front door of Sk8 4Ever jingled their warning that someone was entering the store. Angie looked up to see Cody entering the shop only moments after her friends had left.

"I just saw part of the Wild Bunch in the parking lot," he told Angie with an affectionate chuckle. "Did they buy anything?"

"No. They just stopped by to give me my daily dose of menacing."

Cody looked at her curiously but said

nothing. It was obvious that whatever the skaters had come for was upsetting Angie. But he wasn't one to pry. If she wanted to tell him what was wrong, she would. All in her own time.

Angie was grateful for his restraint. She really didn't want to talk about it.

"All right," Cody said, "I'm going in the back. I've got to screw a new truck into a board for a guy I met in Allentown. If you need anything, let me know."

Angie looked around at the empty store. Things had been busy earlier, but there was a lull now. "I think I can handle the crowd," she joked. "But you'll be happy to know that while you were gone, I sold two sets of pads, that hot pink T-shirt with the black triangle, and a green hoodie."

"Who to?" Cody asked. "Anyone I know?"

"Who do you know who would wear that?" she asked, knowing the answer already. "Just some wannabes."

Cody bit his lip, holding back a smile. "Now, what have I told you about being tolerant of other people?" he asked with mock sternness.

But the seriousness of Angie's response surprised him. "You're right," she replied. "I really have to learn to stop judging people by the size of their wallets."

"Mmmm. Someone's growing up," Cody murmured as he walked into the back of the store.

Ugh. Angie cringed as strains of an old Grateful Dead tune filled the silence in the store from the old tape player Cody kept for himself in the back room. He said he liked the cassettes better than CDs because his best Dead bootlegs were all on tape.

That was one of the downsides of having the store be so empty. When things were busy, Cody let Angie blare her music—it gave the place the ambience the customers expected. But when things were slow, Cody liked to listen to his moldie oldies. She wished Cody could get into her music a little more—maybe play a little Linkin Park or Staind. But Cody had once told her that he'd closed his musical window sometime in the late 1970s, and try as he might, he just couldn't get into the rock and metal the skaters listened to these days. Angie figured his music reminded him of his glory days, back when he was a younger skater boi.

Angie busied herself rehanging the T-shirts and hoodies on the rack. The girls who'd been in earlier had left them all over the floor as they tried on different colors and styles. She was crouched down on the floor picking up a pile of clothing when the bells above the door jingled again.

"Can I help—ow!" Angie stood up to greet the customer, then winced in pain as she banged her head on the metal rack above.

"Whoa, are you okay?" Carter asked, rushing over to help her up.

Angie rubbed the top of her head. An egg-shaped lump was already forming. But she was pretty sure that wasn't the reason for her sudden lightheadedness or the pounding in her chest.

Those were all because of him.

"Chad," she said. "What are you doing here?"

Chad. He frowned slightly. "I came to see you," he told her.

"But how . . . ?"

"I heard Opal mention that you worked here," he reminded her. "Remember? She asked why you couldn't use the airbrush from Sk8 4Ever."

Angie blushed excitedly. He'd really been paying attention that afternoon. He hadn't missed a thing. Then again, neither had she. If she recalled, she'd been checking him out pretty heavily too.

Carter seemed to like the fact that she was blushing, because his warm grin grew even more wide and disarming. "Anyway, I'm here to apologize for, uh, what happened the other night. And cash in my chips."

"Excuse me?"

"You said you'd go to dinner with me again. And you promised to let me pick the restaurant."

Angie took a deep breath. She wasn't so sure that was a good idea. The restaurants he was used to were far out of her league. They probably cost a fortune. And besides, she'd heard stories about guys like him. After they took a girl out and spent a ton of cash on her, they usually expected something in return. "Maybe we could compromise. Go to a movie or something."

Carter shook his head. "No way. This is my turn. Don't worry. All those rumors about my friends and me are greatly exaggerated."

Angie blushed redder. It was like he could read her mind.

"Do your parents get mad if you go out on

school nights?" Carter asked her. "'Cause I was thinking we could go to Chez Français on Wednesday. My trig test'll be over by then, and we can celebrate my just-about passing."

Would my parents get mad? Angie sighed. Her father would probably never even notice— more food for him. Her mother might care, but she'd be too timid and afraid of a confrontation to actually say something. "Nah, they're cool with it," Angie told him finally.

"Good, then it's a date!" Carter exclaimed in a burst of relief that let Angie know he'd been nervous about asking her.

"Why don't you give me your address?" Carter asked her. "I'll pick you up."

Angie fingered the big silver skull-shaped ring on her middle finger nervously. She didn't want him picking her up at her house. Not that she was ashamed of where she lived . . . exactly. Okay, maybe a little. But she was more worried that he'd expect to meet her parents. And while he'd probably be polite, somehow she didn't think he'd click with her beer-guzzling father or her world-weary mother. And for sure they wouldn't like him. There was no reason for them to all meet. It wasn't like this was going to be some lasting thing or anything.

How could it be?

"Look, I have to work Wednesday after school anyway," Angie told him quickly. "Why don't you just pick me up here?"

"Okay," he agreed. "What time do you get off?"

"Six thirty. But I'll need a half an hour to clean up." She regretted the words as soon as they left her mouth. She could just imagine what Buzz and the rest of the gang would've done with an opening like that. They'd probably make some crack about there not being enough hours in the day, or the fact that she'd need a shovel to pack on all the eye makeup she usually wore.

But this guy was different. "Okay. Seven o'clock then. But do me a favor. Don't clean up too much. I like you this way."

Angie didn't know how to answer that. Instead, she studied him for a moment. She was surprised at how much she liked him just the way he was too. Not that she was thrilled with his choice of clothing. Suddenly she was glad Cody was in the back room with the Dead cranked up loud. She doubted he'd appreciate the A&F Henley shirt and Puma sneakers this boy was wearing. Cody had a real grudge against big-name companies and the people who wore their stuff. Usually Angie did too.

But Chad had an amazing smile, and that twinkle in his eyes was irresistible. She had to fight the urge to brush back his straight, boyish blond bangs from his eyes.

"Well, I guess I should be going," Carter said, suddenly seeming uncomfortable under her gaze. He looked out the window for a moment.

Angie nodded. "Don't worry, the coast's clear. They left a little while ago."

"I wasn't worried about—"

"Yes you were," Angie told him. "And I don't blame you. Buzz and Zack can be real jerks sometimes. I'm sorry about your car. *Again.*"

"It's in the shop right now, but I promise it'll be fixed by Wednesday. I rode my bike here."

"The one you earned the cash for being a busboy?"

Carter nodded. "She's my baby. A real beaut. Take a look."

Angie followed him to the shop door and looked out into the parking lot. Sure enough, a sleek motorcycle with a helmet slung over its steering was parked there. It sparkled in the sunlight. Obviously this was a well-loved mode of transportation.

"Would you believe I've never been on a motorcycle?" Angie hinted.

Carter looked at her, surprised. "A girl like you?"

"I don't know anyone who can afford one," she admitted without apology. "The only wheels my friends have are attached to a skateboard deck."

"I'll take you on mine one day if you'd like."

"One day?" Angie asked. She was tired of dropping hints. Obviously she was going to have to be more direct. "What's wrong with now?"

"Well, for starters, you're working. Secondly, I only have one helmet."

Angie walked over to a display of skateboard helmets and pulled a glittery black one off the shelf. "One problem solved," she told him confidently. "Cody, you mind if I take my break now?" she shouted toward the back of the store.

The music became quieter as Cody lowered the volume. "Sure, it's pretty quiet. Just be back in forty-five minutes. I'm expecting a delivery."

"You got it, boss," Angie told him. She smiled at Carter. "Second problem solved."

Carter kicked at the ground for a minute. "Well, I . . . I mean . . . you've never been on a bike?" he asked her again.

"What's the matter, Chad? You afraid I might hurt your precious Honda?"

He looked uncomfortable again. "Okay, you guilted me into it," he said slowly.

"Guilted? How'd I do that?"

"Oh, never mind. Come on. Put your helmet on."

Angie snapped the helmet into place and followed him out into the parking lot. She watched carefully as he climbed onto the front of the bike.

"Okay, get on and wrap your arms around me," Carter told her. "The secret is to move your body into the turns. Your first reaction might be to bend against the turn. But don't do that. Just follow my lead and do what I tell you."

Do what I tell you. If Buzz or one of the other skaters had ordered her to do that, she would have killed them. But she wasn't at all insulted now. She was just thrilled to be sitting here, on the back of a motorcycle, with her arms and legs wrapped tightly around this incredibly adorable boy.

The bike bounced up and down slightly as he turned the motor on, and then they were off. Angie gasped as the cool fall wind slapped her hard in the face. But she soon got used to the feeling. It didn't take long for it all to seem completely natural—comfortable, even. In some ways, riding along on the back of a motorcycle didn't feel all that different from skateboarding. It was the same freedom and excitement—in fact, the very speed of the bike actually enhanced those emotions. She began to revel in the feeling of superiority she felt as they passed by the other drivers on the road, the ones trapped in those metal cages they called cars.

She hugged him tighter, finding herself excited by the nearness of their bodies. Her heart pounded even more fiercely, and she felt a strange tingling in her limbs. She wasn't sure if it was the feeling of driving on the open road, or the way his body felt against hers. She buried her face in the soft spot at the back of his neck, and let herself savor the scent of his aftershave. Like everything else about him, the way he smelled seemed foreign, intriguing, and excitingly forbidden. This was probably the first guy she'd ever known who actually wore cologne. The way the skater guys smelled could only be called *eau de sweat*.

She committed his scent to memory, not wanting to forget a single detail about how she felt at this very moment. Not that she could ever forget. For the rest of her life she would remember the wind blowing wildly around her, the vibrations of the motorcycle against her legs, and the pounding of her heart.

Angie was so lost in thought that she was both surprised and disappointed when Carter pulled the bike back into the parking lot outside Sk8 4Ever. "Can't we ride a little longer?" she begged as she watched him swing his leg over the side of the bike and hop off onto the asphalt below.

Carter pointed to the gold watch on his wrist. "Forty-five minutes. That's all your boss gave you," he reminded her.

Forty-five minutes. Had it really been that long? It seemed like seconds. "Oh, Cody won't mind," Angie assured him. "Let's ride some more. It was so much fun. I'm not ready to go back to work."

"Uh-oh, I think you've caught it," Carter joked. "I knew it was contagious."

"Caught what?"

"The bug."

"What bug?"

"The bike bug. Once you've been on a motorcycle, there's no turning back. You'll never want to travel any other way."

"So let's go again," Angie demanded, refusing to move from the back of the seat.

"No way," Carter replied. "I'm not getting you in trouble. I'd like to stay on your boss's good side."

Angie smirked. "You're such a brown-noser." Carter reached out his hand to help her off the bike, but she shook her head vehemently. "I can do it myself."

She swung her leg over the side of the bike, trying to imitate what she'd seen Carter do. But she wasn't used to the motion, and as she hopped off the bike, her heel caught the seat. *Wham*. The next thing she knew, the bike was on top of her.

"Are you okay?" Carter exclaimed as he hurried to remove the motorcycle from on top of her hip and righted it. "Here ya go. Now, don't try to move if it hurts too much. I can call someone. An ambulance, maybe?" He sounded really frightened and concerned as he flopped down onto the ground beside her and tried to assess her injuries.

Angie sat up slowly and then scrambled to her feet. "I'm fine," she assured him, rubbing her hip gently. "Just gotta walk it off." She moved around the parking lot, trying to shake off the embarrassment, which was actually more painful than the red spot on her hip. "Good thing we were standing still. I could've really been hurt if we were moving. As it is, I'm just a little sore is all."

Carter nodded without actually looking up. He was busy studying every inch of his bike, making sure that nothing was dented or broken. Angie smiled. He wasn't so different from the skaters after all. If she'd slammed on one of their boards, they'd have reacted the same way. At least Chad had had the decency to ask her if she was okay before he checked out his motorcycle. Buzz, Zack, or George wouldn't have bothered. They would've just left her there on the ground while they hurried off to get their boards fixed by Cody or someone.

"You know, you're a menace when it comes to modes of transportation," Carter teased, relaxing once he realized that both Angie and the bike were fine. "First you pound my car, now you knock over my bike. I think we should take the *bus* to Chez Français."

"That's cool," Angie told him sincerely. "I don't mind."

"I'm only kidding," Carter assured her. "My car'll be out of the shop by then. Still, just to be safe, maybe I should rent a tank for the evening. I don't think you can do much damage to one of them."

"You never know," Angie teased back. "Hurricane Angie can be pretty powerful."

Carter smiled, obviously appreciating a girl who was willing to laugh at herself. "Oh, I believe it," he told her. "I've fallen victim to her already." His voice took on a softer tone, one which sent a shiver up her spine. She moved closer to him, anxious to feel the closeness of his body again, to feel his lips on hers, to breathe in his scent. . . .

"Hey, Angie, come on in the back," Cody called out suddenly from the shop's doorway. "The delivery truck's here. I need your help."

"That's my cue," Carter said as he hopped back onto his bike. He pulled on his helmet, turned the key in the ignition, and blew her a kiss. "See ya Wednesday," he shouted over the roar of the engine.

Wednesday! Angie's eyes flew open as he drove away. Quickly she reached into her pocket and pulled out her cell phone. Her fingers flew over the numbers as she hurried to meet Cody behind the skateboard store. As soon as her aunt answered the phone, words flew out of Angie's mouth that she'd never said before. "It's an emergency, Aunt Dodo! *I have nothing to wear!*"

*T*hree o'clock Wednesday afternoon . . . Angie slipped quietly out of the high school and hurried toward the sidewalk, hoping to avoid any of her friends along the way. She didn't feel like having to make up any stupid excuses for not hanging out at the ramp after work this afternoon. And she surely couldn't tell them the truth. It was best to just go to work and try to keep her mind off the growing collection of butterflies in her stomach.

"Yo, Angie." Zack's voice was instantly recognizable as Angie crossed the street. He was standing, or make that *leaning,* up against a stop sign.

"Oh, hey Zack," Angie greeted him, trying to sound as normal as possible. Not that Zack could have picked up any subtle difference in her voice in the state he was in. Angie stepped back. "Whoa. You smell like a brewery. Where've you been?"

"I had a science test last period," Zack explained.

Angie looked at him curiously. "And it was on beer tasting?" she asked sarcastically.

Zack shook his head, missing her sarcasm completely. "I decided not to take it. I've been hangin' out on Senior Hill all afternoon."

Ordinarily, Angie might have wasted some of her breath convincing Zack that that was not the best decision he'd ever made, but today she just wanted to get out of there. "Oh well, hope it was fun. See ya later, Zack." She hurried off in the direction of Sk8 4Ever.

But he wasn't letting her go so easily. "You know, Angie, you're breaking my best dude's heart," he slurred, leaning toward her at such a precarious angle that Angie thought he might fall at any moment.

"Come on, Zack," Angie said, trying to laugh it off. "Buzz has no heart."

Zack tried to focus his eyes on hers. "You know that's not true. He's totally into you. And you just keep blowin' him off. First for your art. Okay, maybe he can handle that. But for a preppie dude? Angie, that's so harsh."

Angie gulped. Was it possible Zack knew about her date with Chad tonight? How could he have . . . ? "I don't know what you're talking about," she said quickly. Maybe too quickly.

"I don't either," Zack admitted. "LeeAnn told me the guy was history. But Buzz, he just can't stop thinking about it."

Angie breathed a sigh of relief. Zack didn't know anything about Chad's visit to the shop or about their date tonight. "Hey, I know how you can take Buzz's mind off of me," she suggested cheerfully. "Tell him about Christie Statesman. I heard puberty finally paid her a call over the summer. She's got huge ones now. She's only a sophomore, but those young girls just worship Buzz, y'know?"

Zack laughed slightly. "You're cold, you know that?" He wrapped his arms around his stomach. "Oh man. I don't feel so good." He leaned his head over the grass and promptly threw up.

Angie leaped out of the way. The last thing she needed was to smell like thrown-up beer when she went out with Chad tonight. She looked down at the ground. Zack was finished retching. He was just sitting there, staring at grass and moaning slightly. She couldn't just leave him there. But she had to get to work. Frantically, she watched the front door of the school, hoping one of their gang would come into her view and be willing to take over on Zack-watch.

Just then, LeeAnn and Gina emerged from the building. *Thank God.* Angie waved her arms frantically in their direction. "Yo, you guys. C'mere!" she shouted as loud as she could, hoping they'd hear her over the traffic.

Sure enough, LeeAnn and Gina crossed the street. LeeAnn looked down and sighed bitterly. "There he is, ladies. The man of my dreams."

"He bagged the science test and hung out on Senior Hill with his pal Bud Weiser." Angie explained. "Listen, you guys, I've gotta get to work. Can you take over here?"

"No prob," LeeAnn agreed. "Zack yack—I've been this route a million times. Gina, go back to school and get paper towels. Some wet, some dry." She reached into the front pocket of her backpack and pulled out a lint-covered Life Saver. "Put this in your mouth," she ordered Zack. "I'm not coming within ten feet of you till ya do."

"Thanks," Angie told her girlfriends sincerely.

"Are you coming to the ramp after work?" Gina asked as she waited for the light to change.

Angie shook her head. "No. Gotta work on my French." She cringed inwardly. It wasn't exactly a lie. She *was* going to a French restaurant, after all.

"French. Like that's going to do you any good around here," Gina said.

"She's not staying here, remember?" Zack reminded her in a voice tinged with dizziness, envy, and resentment. "Angie's too good for Torren."

"I'm not too good for—,"Angie began.

"Forget it, Ange," LeeAnn said quietly. "It's just the brew talkin'. Get out of here before you're late for work."

Angie wasn't sure if LeeAnn had suddenly sounded distant, or if she'd imagined it because she felt so guilty about lying to her pals. Either way, it wasn't a good feeling. "Thanks again," she said as she headed down the road toward the skateboard store.

Five o'clock Wednesday afternoon . . .
Angie sensed Cody staring at her behind her back. She turned slowly and stuck her tongue out at him playfully. "What?" she demanded.

"Nothing," he said quietly. "Why?"

"You were staring at me."

"Oh, that," Cody said. "I guess I was wondering why you've been dropping things all afternoon."

Oops. Angie stood up too soon and knocked over a pile of metal trucks. "You mean like that?" She bent down to pick up the small metal squares.

"Exactly." Cody chuckled.

"I'm just kind of nervous," Angie admitted.

"About the mysterious big event tonight?" Cody asked. "The one you need to use my back office as a dressing room for?"

Angie nodded. "It's a date, actually."

"Oh," Cody said, trying hard not to pry.

"With a guy you don't know."

"Mmm," Cody replied. "I'm sure you'll have a good time."

"I hope so," Angie began. She took a deep breath. Cody would be a good person to talk to about this whole thing with Chad. He was pretty levelheaded. On the other hand, he'd been a skater and a surfer, and he was pretty loyal to his own kind. Still, sometimes he had good advice. "He's not like us, you know."

"He's not?"

Angie shook her head. "He's different."

"What?" Cody asked her with mock concern. "He's not human? Are you dating a dog, Angie?"

Good old Cody. He always made everything easier. "No, I just mean he's not a skater or anything. He's sort of rich."

"Oh."

"But he's different than the rest of them."

Cody nodded slowly and ran one of his well-worn hands over his thick beard. "You've met the rest of them?" he asked calmly.

"No. I mean, he's rich, but he's not a loser."

"Well, I'm glad to hear that."

Angie sighed heavily. "You know what I'm talking about."

"I think I do, and I'm disappointed in you, kiddo."

Her face fell. "I knew you would be. What was I thinking? Me going to some fancy restaurant with a rich brat. What a sellout I am. Everyone'll be mad if I go out with him. I should probably just stand him up. Forget the whole thing."

Cody walked over and put a strong arm around Angie's shoulder. "No, don't do that. I'm not disappointed that you're going out with

109

this kid. I'm disappointed that you're so prejudiced."

"Me? Prejudiced? What are you talking
about? I never said *anything* about his race."

"Prejudiced means to prejudge. You're pre-
judging these kids just 'cause they're rich."

"Well, they prejudge us."

"Oh yeah," Cody said slowly. "I forgot. Two
wrongs make a right."

Angie groaned under her breath. "You
know what I mean."

"I do. And I know that making judgments
about people based on how they dress, what
kind of cars they drive, or what they choose to
do for a living isn't just shallow. It's cruel. And
it drives people apart. *Sometimes forever.*"

There was an icy coldness in Cody's voice
Angie hadn't heard before. "You know, it's a
funny thing about people," Cody continued.
"They're kind of like apples. They're all different
kinds, but most of them are pretty sweet. Can't
judge any of 'em by the few that are wormy."

Angie looked at him strangely for a
moment, taking it all in. Then she opened her
mouth and pretended to gag on her forefinger.
"Oh please," she moaned. "That's the lamest
thing I've ever heard."

Cody gave her a big wink. "What, you think all old guys with beards are philosophers?" he asked her, laughing. "Look, just go on the date, have a good time, and stop thinking so hard. You've got to learn to let go, Angie."

"But . . ."

"This night is a really high ramp," Cody admitted. "Probably the highest you've ever come up against, because it's challenging everything you've ever thought—about yourself and about those rich kids. Now, you can either go up to the top and let yourself fly, or you can decide it's just too scary and slalom away. Frankly, Angie, I've never seen you chicken out of anything before. Why start now?"

Leave it to Cody to put the whole thing in terms she could relate to. This *was* a big deal. A huge deal. Maybe more than she could actually handle. She was, after all, just a kid. After a moment of consideration she frowned, reached into her pocket, and pulled out her cell phone.

"You're actually going to *cancel* with him?" Cody sounded surprised.

"No," Angie assured him. "I'm calling my aunt Dodo. I want to be sure she remembers to bring her perfume, too."

111

Six o'clock Wednesday evening . . .

 Tick . . . tick . . . tick . . . The sound of the second hand on the big black-and white-clock was really getting on Angie's nerves. It was six o'clock on the dot. Her aunt Dodo had promised she'd be at the shop on time. Not a second late. But now she was ten seconds late . . . eleven . . . twelve . . .

 "Hello, your fashion consultant is here!" Dodo announced as she floated into Sk8 4Ever, bringing her usual burst of energy and a long black suit bag.

 "Oh Aunt Dodo, I thought you weren't coming," Angie said, hugging her tightly.

 Aunt Dodo looked up at the clock on the wall. It read 6:01. She laughed, remembering what it was like to be eighteen. "Why must I be a teenager in love?" she hummed quietly under her breath, recalling an old sixties standard.

 "So, did you find something that would work for me?" Angie begged.

 "Well, you're a lot taller—and trimmer—than I am these days," Aunt Dodo replied, cheerfully slapping her slightly spreading, middle-aged rear end. "But this morning I remembered I'd saved this from back when I

112

was in Madrid. I think you'll like it. It's got plenty of black in it." With a great flourish, she unzipped the bag and whipped out a black lace top.

"Oh I like that," Angie squealed with uncharacteristic excitement.

"That's nothing. Check this out." She removed a long black-and-red floral skirt with black lace trim along the bottom.

"Flowers?" Angie gasped. The words were out of her mouth before she could stop herself.

But Dodo wasn't upset at her niece's reaction. "What did you expect? A leather skirt with silver studs? I thought you were going for something really different."

"This is different, all right," Angie agreed, trying to be as congenial as possible under the circumstances. "I don't really do flowers, that's all."

"Well tonight, *Angela,* you will do flowers," Dodo said, using Angie's full name to provide her with even more sophistication. Then she reached into the pocket of the suit bag and pulled out a pair of sleek black pumps. "And heels!"

"Heels?" Angie's voice scaled up nervously. "Aunt Dodo, I don't know if . . ."

"They're no higher than those Frankenstein boots you tool around in all the time."

"I guess not," Angie mused, pondering the heels of the shoes.

"Anyway, you've no choice. You've got to put this on. I didn't bring anything else." Aunt Dodo smiled triumphantly. "Now go get changed."

"Cody's still in there," Angie said. "I've got to wait until he finishes his paperwork."

"Don't be ridiculous," her aunt replied, darting into the back room.

"You can't just . . ."

But Angie's words were lost on her aunt. Telling her she couldn't do something was an open invitation to have her just do that.

"Okay Cody, evacuate the premises," Angie heard her say. "We ladies are taking over."

"Hello to you too, Dorothy," Cody greeted her.

"No time for small talk. Prince Charming'll be here any minute, and Cinderella had nothing on the rags my niece is wearing right now."

"Hey!" Angie shouted as she stormed into the backroom. "I like these jeans." She pointed to her new black jeans, which had buckles going down the outside of each leg and a thin chain that was connected to the back and front left pockets.

"They're great for doing a feeblegrind, but not for eating at Chez Français," Cody informed her.

Angie and her aunt stared at him in surprise.

"Hey, I'm not a complete fashion moron," Cody informed them.

Dodo studied Cody's worn jeans and bright orange-and-black tie-dyed T-shirt with a huge picture of Jimi Hendrix on the front. "Not a *complete* one," she teased.

"Okay, you girls win." He grabbed his notebook and headed for the door. "I'm leaving before I get any more abuse."

"That's better," Dodo said as she closed the door. She pulled out a large tiger-print makeup bag. "I brought some makeup-removal wipes to take off that heavy eyeliner and lipstick. I think all you need tonight is mascara, a bit of blush, and gloss."

"No way," Angie told her. "I like my makeup. What do you think this is, some sort of *Jenny Jones* show—'Please Make Over My Skater Chick Niece'?"

Aunt Dodo smiled. "Nothing that extreme,

my love. You'll still have those charming red tips in your hair. And be happy I didn't bring a pretty little Laura Ashley dress with a matching headband."

"The eyeliner stays!" Angie put her foot down hard.

Aunt Dodo sighed. "You're so stubborn."

"Gee, wonder which relative I get that from?" Angie replied. She eyed her aunt's flowing red-and-cream-colored gauze Indian skirt, her oversized white blouse, and the red fake pashmina shawl. "I don't see you following the latest trends just to fit in."

"You've got a point. But then again, I'm not the one who asked for help."

There was no arguing with that. "Okay, here's the thing. I don't want to change for anyone. He either likes me for who I am, or he doesn't. I'll wear the floral skirt, but the eyeliner stays."

Aunt Dodo was quiet for a moment. "You know, you're pretty smart for a kid. I guess I did go a little overboard. It just seemed like so much fun to help you play dress-up for a night. Your mom used to write me about how you would traipse around in her shoes and her dresses when you were little. I missed that whole part of your growing up. I suppose I was trying to get a little of it in now."

"I do appreciate your help," Angie said quietly, smiling slightly at the memories of a less complicated time when playing dress-up was all about fun, not about trying to be someone you weren't. "And the top *is* really cool."

"Good." Aunt Dodo gave her a big hug. "The eyeliner stays."

"Thank goodness."

"But what about the lip gloss?"

Angie studied her face in the reflection of the small mirror on the office wall. "I guess that's up for negotiation."

Six-fifty-five Wednesday evening . . .

Angie walked slowly out of the back office, trying hard not to fall in her aunt's black pumps. The heels were small and tippy, but at least she wasn't wearing the awful pantyhose her aunt had tried to insist on. She felt strange and awkward in the flowing skirt. She hadn't worn anything but jeans since elementary school—when she'd first discovered skateboarding.

"You look great, kiddo," Cody said as she emerged.

117

"I look ridiculous."

"No, you *feel* ridiculous," he corrected her. "You *look* amazing. And I bet what's-his-name's gonna think so, too."

"His name is Chad. Chad Montgomery."

"Chad Montgomery?" Aunt Dodo repeated. "Sounds like a soap-opera name."

Cody burst out laughing. "Chad Montgomery, the future husband of Erica Kane."

Now it was Dodo's turn to surrender to a fit of giggles.

Angie scowled at the two of them. "Cut it out."

"Sorry, sweetie, it's just not a name I'm used to, that's all," Aunt Dodo apologized.

"Well, I'm sure Cody and Dodo aren't names *he* hears every day, either."

"You're right," Cody agreed as a pair of bright car lights appeared in the parking lot. "By the way, Mr. Montgomery's chariot has just pulled up."

Angie turned around quickly. For the first time, she knew exactly what the expression "deer caught in the headlights" really meant. Suddenly it all seemed so stupid—the floral skirt, her hair tied up in a bun behind her head, and especially the shoes. What was she thinking? This wasn't her world at all.

But it was too late to do anything about it now. He was here. The bells jingling above the doorway made that abundantly clear.

"Wow!" Carter exclaimed, staring at Angie with surprise. "You look . . ."

"You too," Angie said, noting that he'd put a light gel in his hair to keep the bangs from falling. She stood back and admired his loose-fitting gray-and-black wool sport jacket. No one she knew even owned a jacket like that—except maybe a teacher or two. And none of *them* ever looked this hot in it.

Cody and Aunt Dodo stood off to the side, watching as the two teens stared at each other. "Ahem," Dodo said finally.

"Oh, Aunt Dod . . . *Aunt Dorothy* . . . this is Chad Montgomery," she said. "Chad, this is my aunt, and my boss, Cody."

Cody studied Carter's face curiously. "Montgomery, eh?" he said. "I knew a Tom Montgomery back when I was surfing in Hawaii. Man, could he catch a wave. You any relation?"

"Um, no sir," Carter said quickly.

"You sure?"

"Absolutely."

"Mon Dieu!" Dodo interrupted in frustration. "I'm certain Angie and Chad would love to spend more time talking old times with you, Cody, but I'll bet they have a reservation."

"Yes ma'am," Carter replied gratefully, glancing at his gold watch to check the time.

"Ma'am?" She shook her head. "Please, call me Dodo. Angie always has, ever since she was a baby."

Angie frowned. *How embarrassing.* Did her aunt have to reveal all of their family secrets?

But Carter seemed to like her aunt's nickname. "Dodo," he repeated. "I like that. You know, I have a great-aunt Dorothy on my father's side."

"Oh, what do you call her?" Dodo asked him.

"Aunt Dorothy."

"Of course you do," Cody butted in. "She'd never settle for anything else."

Angie looked at him curiously. "How would you know?"

"Just an educated guess. I had an aunt like that once." Cody shot her an encouraging smile. "Now get out of here before I decide to make you stay and help me with inventory."

"Have fun, *cheries,*" Aunt Dodo said as they left.

The two adults watched as the teens walked off into the parking lot. "Chad Montgomery," Cody said aloud. "I don't know about him."

"What?" Dodo asked. "He seemed nice enough to me."

"I just think there's something he's not telling her. I don't know what it is. Just a feeling I have."

Dodo shook her head and gave him a playful shove. "Sorry, pal, I'm the one with the intuitive feelings. Stay out of my line of work. You don't see me putting together skateboards, do you?"

"So what's your prediction? Do you think it'll go okay tonight?"

"It won't be anything Angie can't handle."

"You get positive vibes from that boy?"

Dodo thought for a moment, considering the first impression she'd received from him. "I think he's a good guy. And he honestly likes Angie. He's a bit of a rebel, I think . . . which is something you and I can definitely appreciate."

Cody gave her a conspiratorial grin. They were truly two of a kind.

"But as for *secrets* . . . ," Dodo continued. "I think we've all got parts of our past we'd rather not claim as our own. Don't you, Cody?"

He looked at her curiously, but said nothing.

"So how well do you know Cody?" Carter asked as he and Angie walked toward his car. Well, *he* walked. She sort of stumbled around on her aunt's high heels, hoping he didn't notice how unused to the shoes she was.

"Pretty well. We work together a few afternoons a week and on Saturdays."

"But I mean, where's he from? Around here?"

Angie shook her head. "I don't think so. He's traveled around a lot, doing skating and surfing comps. He just came to town a few years ago. Why?"

"It's just that there's something familiar about him."

"What?"

"I don't know. I feel like I know him or something."

"I can't imagine where you would've seen him. He hasn't competed for a long time. So even if he was in some skateboard or surfing magazine . . ."

"Yeah, you're probably right," Carter agreed, as he buckled his seat belt and turned the key in the ignition.

"Could you put the top down while we drive?" Angie pleaded, sounding very much like a little kid asking for a Popsicle from the ice cream truck.

He looked at her strangely. "We're going on the highway, you know."

"Sure. Isn't that why you get a convertible? So you can feel the wind on your face?"

"Aren't you worried about your hair?"

"Why would I worry about that?" she replied with surprise. "Who cares? I can always tie it up again."

Carter eyed her appreciatively. "You're going to take a little getting used to," he admitted. "But it's going to be a lot of fun." He flicked a switch on the dashboard and the roof of the car immediately slid back.

Angie leaned comfortably against the rich leather seat and looked up at the sky. It was a clear night with a three-quarter moon. Already, the first few stars had started to appear. She was oddly disappointed that she'd missed that first star. There were definitely a few wishes she could've made tonight.

"You cold?" Carter shouted over the crisp fall wind that blew all around them.

Angie shook her head.

"Because you can wear my jacket if—"

"I'm fine, Chad," she said loudly.

Carter grimaced. "Angie . . . about that *Chad* thing. I'm not . . ."

"What?" she asked, shouting over the wind. "I can't hear you."

"Never mind," he said, losing his nerve.

Chez Français was quiet. Wednesday night wasn't their busiest time of the week. Still, there were a few people in the restaurant, all adults—men in business suits and women in chic dresses and shoes. *Well, chic for Torren, anyway,* Angie thought to herself. Any place known for its terry cloth wasn't going to get a write-up in any fashion magazine real soon.

"Why don't you sit here in the lounge, and I'll go ask the maître d' if our table's ready," Carter suggested, guiding Angie to a little round table in the bar area of the restaurant.

"I can just go with you."

"No, you relax. I don't want you to have to walk any more than you have to in those things. They must be really uncomfortable." He glanced down at Angie's high heels.

She blushed deeply. So he had noticed. "Okay," she said, taking a seat. She watched him walk away, and then looked around the room. Suddenly she felt very conspicuous. She was probably the only one in the entire lounge under the age of forty, and she was *definitely* the only one with bright red tips in her hair. Usually being different from the uptight business types would've been a badge of honor for Angie. But tonight she just felt out of place. They were on his turf, and she didn't feel at all comfortable with the shift in power.

She watched as the maître d' greeted her date like an old friend. They chatted for a while, and then the maître d' nodded. Within a few seconds, Carter was back at her side.

"It's ready," he said, helping Angie to her feet and holding her arm while she steadied herself on the heels. "I asked him for one near the fireplace."

"That sounds nice," Angie said concentrating hard on not falling as they walked all the way to the back of the restaurant. As they reached their table, Angie pulled out her chair and sat down, not realizing she was leaving the befuddled maître d' standing there, his arms extended to pull the chair out for her.

"Do you come to this place a lot?" Angie asked as she placed the napkin on her lap and looked at all the spoons and forks in front of her. She wasn't quite sure which one was for what, but she figured she'd just follow his lead.

"Not too often. Every once in a while. But they really do make the best French food. And I figured you might like to try . . ."

"I love French food," Angie assured him.

"You've had it before?" He sounded suprised and slightly disappointed.

"Sure. French fries, eat 'em all the time." She grinned at the expression on his face. "*I'm kidding.* My aunt Dodo used to live in Paris and she's made a few things for me. I haven't eaten a whole lot of French food, though." She scanned the menu, looking a bit overwhelmed. "You know, this place seems pretty expensive. I would've been happy with a hamburger and fries."

"No. I want this night to be special," Carter insisted.

"But I *like* burgers and fries."

"Would you like me to order for you?" he asked her. "I know it's confusing since the whole menu is in French."

"Sure, go for it," Angie agreed, closing her menu. "My appetite is in your hands."

Carter waved his hand toward the waiter. "Garçon," he called in an accent that smacked of high-school French.

"Oui, monsieur?"

"We're ready to order," Carter told him. "I think we'll both start with the soup du jour." He looked at Angie. "It's onion soup, okay?"

Angie nodded.

"Good," Carter replied. He was doing his best to sound sophisticated. "Then, I think for a main course, we'll try the *cervelle de mouton*."

The waiter looked at him skeptically, but scribbled down the order.

"Boy, I'm impressed," Angie remarked with a raised eyebrow. "You're really adventurous."

"What do you mean?" Carter asked her, insulted at her implication.

"Well, it's not everyone who'll order sheep's brains for dinner."

Carter almost gagged. "Sheep's brains?"

"You did say *cervelle de mouton*, didn't you?"

"Yes. But isn't that . . ."

"Sheep's brains," the waiter translated for him. "She's right."

"How about I order for us?" Angie suggested.

Carter nodded, too embarrassed to say anything.

"We'll each have an order of *boeuf et pommes frites*," she told the waiter. "Medium rare."

As the waiter walked away, Carter shook his head. "You speak French."

Angie nodded.

"How come you didn't tell me?"

"You didn't ask."

Carter's embarrassment turned to amusement. He couldn't help but laugh at his own behavior. "Okay, you got me."

"I sure did," Angie agreed. "But you deserved it. What made you think I couldn't order for myself?"

"I don't know what I was thinking. But I promise never to assume anything like that again. I've got to be on my toes around you."

"You know it, buster," she agreed.

"So, how's the art portfolio coming?" Carter asked, eager to change the subject.

"It's pretty much done. So's my application. I'm just waiting for my parents to fill out their part of the financial aid forms. They've been putting it off. I guess they just don't like asking for help."

"Apple doesn't fall far, does it?" he suggested pointedly.

Angie cringed a bit, remembering the first

time they'd met. "It's not the same thing," she insisted. "This isn't some little airbrush I'm trying to get. My entire future's riding on this. And they're letting their pride get in the way of me getting out of Torren. I swear, they're so selfish!"

"You really hate Torren, don't you?"

"You would too, if you were in my situation. It's different here for someone like me. If I stay, my future's a done deal. And it's not a pretty picture. Job at the mill, raising a bunch of brats, all of whom will grow up to work at the mill just like their grandparents and their parents." She took a gulp of her water. "I know that must sound really weird to you."

"Don't be so sure," Carter argued. "I don't want to spend my whole life here either. I'd love to get out right after graduation. Go to college somewhere in New York, Chicago, maybe L.A., and never come back. I'm thinking about going to law school. Actually, I don't care what I major in, as long as it gets me out of town. To me, college's a one-way ticket away from winding up just like my father."

"What's wrong with your father?" Angie asked.

"Hell, I've seen what life in Torren's done

to him. He's got no imagination, no soul left. He's just a drone."

"Sounds like our dads have a lot in common," Angie murmured. "Except your dad's probably a drone with a fancy office and a big car. My dad's a drone on the loading dock at Morgan Mills, with a used '87 Oldsmobile."

Carter got quiet.

"What's your dad do, anyway?" Angie asked curiously.

"He . . . um . . . he's working in the family business. Nothing special."

"What kind of business is that?"

Carter took a big sip of water, and sat back, thinking. But before he could explain anything, the waiter appeared with two large plates, each with a shiny silver rounded cover.

"Your *boeuf et pomme frites,*" the waiter told them as he placed the plates on the table. "Medium rare." He removed the covers with great flare.

Carter stared at his plate for a moment, and then burst out laughing. "Hamburgers and French fries?" he asked her with disbelief.

"Actually, it's more of a chopped steak, sir," the waiter explained.

"Thus the lack of a bun," Angie added,

grinning. "Probably not as good as at Hamburger Heaven, but . . ." She took a bite of a thick steak fry. "Pretty yummy."

"Can I get you anything else?" the waiter asked, clearly enjoying Carter's reaction to Angie's little joke.

"No, I think we're fine," Carter said, cutting into his burger. "Or at least I am. How about you, Ange?"

"Oh I couldn't be better." She placed a forkful of meat into her mouth and chewed happily. "I just love burgers and fries."

"You're pretty proud of yourself, aren't you?" Carter teased.

"You have no idea." She took another triumphant bite. "One way or another, I always get what I want."

By the time the meal was over, Angie no longer felt like a stranger on a rich boy's turf. In fact, she was barely even aware of anyone else in the restaurant. It was just the two of them, as comfortable as a couple could be. Already they were sharing private jokes about his C minus in seventh-grade French, and her custom Strawberry Shortcake boards. And despite their differences, there didn't seem to be any topic they couldn't touch on. She couldn't wait to fill this stranger in on her most secret hopes and passions. And he seemed to feel the same way. They listened to each other without judgment.

A sea of disappointment washed over Angie as the waiter brought the check to their table. She felt like Cinderella at midnight—wishing she could have just one more minute with this handsome stranger, knowing that as soon as they walked out the door she'd be right back in the dismal reality that was her life in Torren.

Angie took a deep breath as they exited into the parking a lot. A crowd of wealthy kids had gathered there. For some reason, they seemed to be hanging around the silver Beetle convertible.

"See, I told you C. M. was here," a tall, thin, dark-haired preppie in a bright blue polo shirt told the others. "I'd know my best friend's sweet car anywhere."

"But you didn't tell us he had a *date,* Ted," one of the girls reminded him. She swung her long blond hair over her shoulder and looked Angie up and down disapprovingly.

"I didn't know," Ted remarked pointedly. He stared at his best buddy.

Ted's comment wasn't lost on Angie. So

Chad hadn't mentioned her to his friends. Well, she couldn't really get too mad at that. It wasn't like she'd volunteered the information about her date tonight to her crowd either.

"What're you guys doing here?" Carter asked the crowd nervously.

"We were hanging out at Jackson's," the blond girl replied, pointing to a lanky red-headed boy who was wearing a prep school varsity letter jacket. "But his 'rents arrived back unexpectedly. So we left. We were heading over to the club when we spotted your car here."

"I guess you won't be coming with us," Ted said.

"Why not?" Carter questioned him.

The preppies looked slightly uncomfortable. Angie didn't feel any more relaxed than they did. Only Carter seemed perfectly okay with the situation.

"Well, it's not that we don't want you, C. M.," Ted said. "It's just that, well . . . you know . . . it's the *club*. You have to be a member to get in."

"I can bring a guest any time I want. Any of us can."

"But C. M.," Ted began. "I think my folks are there. You wouldn't want . . ."

The blond girl laughed quietly under her breath and turned to a small brunette in soft gray wool slacks and a tight pink cashmere sweater. "Can't you just see their faces if he walked in with *her*?" she whispered, just loud enough for Angie to hear. "The whole club would be buzzing with it. Carter Morgan III and his juvenile-delinquent date. Oh, that's too much." She laughed again.

Carter Morgan III? Angie shook her head. Was it possible she'd heard wrong? Could the snotty blonde have been talking about someone else? Surely she couldn't have been talking about Chad. Not *Chad Montgomery.*

She thought for a moment. What was it Ted had called him? Oh right, *C. M.* But that could stand for Chad Montgomery.

It could also stand for Carter Morgan.

Angie turned to him, praying that it was all some mistake, but knowing it wasn't. "Chad?" she asked, her eyes pleading.

The rich kids looked from Angie to Carter with surprise. *"Chad?"* Jackson asked. "What's that about?"

"Yeah, what's *that* about?" Angie seconded, her voice growing angrier with each passing second.

Carter bit his lip and kicked at the ground. He looked longingly into her eyes. "Angie, I was going to tell you . . ."

"He gave her a fake name," Ted guffawed. He slapped Carter on the back. "Good move, pal. I guess you were gonna pay the motel man in cash then, huh? It doesn't say Chad on your credit card."

"You think they're going to a motel?" the cashmere-clad brunette sounded incredulous.

"Sure," Ted snarled. "You know what skater chicks are like. Why else would he have bought her an expensive dinner like that?" He spoke about Angie as though she wasn't there.

She took a deep breath. Her head was spinning. She didn't know who to be angrier at—Ted, who was practically calling her a whore to her face, or Carter, the uberjerk, who'd lied to her about his name and God knows what else. Suddenly she was filled with an overflowing wave of hatred and frustration that she could no longer control. In her wild furor, she reached out her fist and swung, hoping to get at least one of them. Better yet, both of them!

Her fist reached at least one mark, landing squarely in the center of Ted's stomach. He doubled over in pain. "You bitch!" he shouted, coughing painfully. Then he lifted his head slightly and glared up at Carter. "C. M., what kind of trash are you slumming with, anyway?"

"You should be happy it was her and not me that hit you," Carter told him. "My right hook's a lot stronger."

"*You* should be happy I got him and not you, *Carter Morgan*." Angie spat the name out as thought it were hot pepper on her tongue. "You lying scum."

"I was going to tell you, Angie. I *tried* to."

"You didn't try hard enough. Better yet, you could've told me the truth from the beginning."

"Would you have gone out with me if you knew my grandfather owned the mill your dad worked in? Or that it was my family that was trying to block your boss's skatepark?" Carter demanded.

"No," Angie told him. "I wouldn't have dated you. I wouldn't even have spoken to you. And I would've saved us both a whole lot of time."

Carter looked over at his friends. They were all staring at him in amazement. "Why don't you take a picture?" he asked, repeating what Angie had said to him at Opal's. "It'll last longer."

"Whoa, you'd better be careful, C. M.," Jackson warned. "You're starting to sound like one of them."

Carter ignored his comment. "Come on, Angie, let's get out of here. We should go someplace private where we can talk."

"I want to go home." Her voice was breaking, but she held back the tears. There was no way she was crying in front of them.

He walked around and opened the passenger-side door. "Fine. Get in. I'll take you."

"No thank you. I'm not going anywhere with you." Angie's eyes were small and bitter. "I can walk. It's not *that* far to my side of the tracks from here."

Actually, it was pretty far to Angie's house from Chez Français. Especially in high heels. By the time she reached her house, she had a few really grody blisters on her toes.

Great, she thought bitterly. *I probably won't be able to skateboard tomorrow. This night just keeps getting better and better.*

Dodo was sitting on the steps outside the house smoking one of her awful-smelling herbal cigarettes when Angie hobbled up.

"*Mon Dieu!* What happened to you?" she asked with concern as Angie collapsed into a tired heap beside her on the step.

"This was the worst night of my entire life, Aunt Dodo," Angie cried. "Do you know who I was out with tonight?"

"Chad Montgomery?"

Angie shook her head vehemently. "No. There is no Chad Montgomery. His real name is Carter Morgan III, as in the son of Carter Morgan II, as in the grandson of Carter Morgan, owner of Morgan Mills."

Dodo nodded her head slowly. "So that's his secret," she murmured.

"You knew?" Angie was incredulous. "Why did you let me go out with him?"

"I knew there was something he was holding back, but I couldn't figure it out. Cody knew it too."

"Can you imagine? I shared a meal—no, make that *two* meals—with the grandson of the man who has condemned my father and half the men in this town to a life of . . ."

"Whoa, stop right there," Dodo said, stamping out her cigarette butt on the floor. "No one condemned your dad to anything. He chose to work at the mill. They all did."

"They had no choice, and you know it. There's no way out of Torren."

"There's always a choice, *ma cherie*."

"Well, anyway, he lied to me. And I can't stand that."

"Angie, look at me," Dodo said softly. "Before you found out the name his parents bestowed on him at birth, did you like the guy?"

Angie nodded. "Pretty stupid of me, huh?"

"No. Pretty human of you. He seems like a nice kid. Besides . . ."

Before Dodo could finish her sentence, Angie's cell phone rang. She took the phone from her purse and clicked on the answer button. "Hello?"

"Angie, it's me, Buzz."

She sighed. She wasn't in the mood for him right now. "I can't talk, Buzz. Tomorrow—"

"Wait. Ange, please don't hang up. I'm in trouble."

"What's wrong?" she asked with genuine concern.

"I'm down at the sheriff's office. I've been arrested."

"Oh Buzz, what've you done now?"

"Nothing, Ange, I swear. I was just skating on the loading dock behind the mill. There was no one there. I wasn't bothering anybody. But Sheriff Martin came by and busted me."

"Were you drinking?"

"No," Buzz vowed. "Honest."

"So what did he say? Did he charge you with trespassing?"

"Geez, don't give him any ideas," Buzz replied. "He could be listening in on the other line."

"So what'd he get you on?" Angie asked. She was getting tired of this guessing game.

"You're not going to believe this," Buzz replied. "He arrested me for skateboarding without a helmet."

"There's no law against that," Angie said.

"There is now. The town council passed it at a meeting last week. It was Carter Morgan's idea. He'll do anything to get us in trouble. I don't know what the old fart has against skaters, but he's sure got it in for us. Anyhow, I gotta pay a twenty-five dollar fine or I'm spending the night in the town jail. Angie, I don't have any money."

Carter Morgan. Just the mention of the name got Angie's blood boiling. "He's an asshole," she groused. "The whole damn family's full of them!"

141

"What are you talking about?" Buzz asked. "Oh look, never mind. I just need the money. You were the only one I could think to call. If I called my old man to come get me . . . well, you know . . ."

Angie sighed. She knew all too well. Buzz's dad had a hair-trigger temper. If he found out Buzz was in jail, he'd beat the crap out of him. Mr. McGrath was a big guy. Buzz would have better luck with the career criminals in jail.

"Don't worry, I'm on my way," Angie told him. "I'll get you out."

"You won't tell your parents, willya, Angie? If your dad spoke to my dad . . ." Buzz suddenly sounded small and afraid. The tone in his voice melted Angie's heart.

"I'll never tell them. I swear, Buzz."

She hung up the phone and started for the front door.

"Where are you going?"

"I gotta go help Buzz out of a jam," she told Dodo. "Thanks to Carter Morgan III's beloved grandpa, he's in jail—for doing nothing. I've got to go pay a twenty-five dollar fine and get him out of there." She looked down at her aunt's clothes and shoes. "I can't let Buzz see me dressed like this. He'd think I'd gone crazy."

She stood up and headed toward the house. "I'm not sure I wasn't crazy tonight. But it's okay. I'm sane again. And I'll never speak to that jerk Carter again!"

"Angie, think about what you're giving up by ending this thing with Carter Morgan. And I don't mean the money or the fancy restaurants. I'm talking about things that matter. Whether he's Carter, Chad, or Bozo, that guy's nuts about you. He may have made a few mistakes, but he understands you in a way Buzz and the others never will."

"Yeah, right. Carter Morgan III understands me. How could someone from his family possibly do that?"

Dodo sighed. "He can't help who his family is, Angie. That's something none of us choose. Our only choice is to follow our own hearts and rise above the sins of our fathers. Hey, what's a name anyway? Remember, a rose by any other name would smell as sweet."

Angie shook her head. "And stinkweed by any other name would still *stink*!" She walked into the dark, cluttered house and let the door slam shut behind her.

143

9

Angie woke up with a wicked headache on Thursday morning. Her stomach felt pretty lousy too. *Something didn't agree with me,* she thought ruefully as she threw on a pair of baggy black pants and a tight T-shirt with a black widow spider emblazoned on the front. She looked over at the desk chair where her aunt's skirt and blouse lay in a heap. *Hell, the whole night didn't agree with me.* She finished getting dressed, brushed her teeth and hair, and clomped her way downstairs.

"Good morning, Angie," Sally Simms greeted her only child. "Want some eggs?"

Angie's stomach rolled at the thought. "No thanks, Mom. I'll grab something on the way." She took her skateboard from the closet, threw her backpack over her shoulder, and skated off toward school.

As she slalomed around trees, mailboxes, and trash cans, Angie tried to push Carter Morgan III from her memory. But the anger was too fresh for her to just let it fly away. The blisters on her feet were a pretty constant memory too.

Angie reached the school just before the first bell rang. She stood on the sidewalk for a moment, watching the kids as they raced into the building. She had math first period today. It was all the way on the fifth floor. She'd have to hurry if she was going to get there on time. But Angie didn't move. Somehow she didn't think she could face a board full of theorems and equations feeling the way she did. In fact, there was only one place she wanted—no, make that *needed*—to be right now. She flipped her skateboard around and headed off toward the ramp.

The empty lot where the makeshift ramp stood was completely deserted. That was just what Angie had been hoping for. She wasn't in the mood to listen to a bunch of stupid skater arguments, like whether or not Avril Lavigne had sold out skaters by letting some rich producers turn her "Sk8er Boi" song into a Hollywood movie.

She went to the top of the ramp at top speed. As she reached the lip, she flew off, using her body to turn herself three hundred and sixty degrees in midair. The wind raced through her hair and she closed her eyes for a second, enjoying the feeling of utter solitude. She landed lightly and rocked back and forth up and down the ramp. As the board came to a stop, she took a deep breath, and realized for the first time that she'd been crying as she'd done her bigspin.

The tears came faster and more furiously as she went back to the top of the ramp and flew off again, this time soaring higher than she had before and pushing herself to turn faster. The release was magical. Angie felt lighter than air. The horrors of the night before seemed to be blown away by the fall wind that followed her as she rode her board. Over and over again, she went up to the top of the ramp and flew.

Some people might have been afraid of the distance between the top of the ramp and the ground below. But not Angie. She was most comfortable when she was flying through the air. At the ramp she never second-guessed herself; she never had to try to be someone she wasn't. This was where she belonged.

"Nice move."

Angie turned around suddenly, realizing that Buzz had been watching her from beside a nearby tree. She wondered how long he'd been standing there. "Thanks," she said, quickly rubbing away any residual tears.

"Thought you'd be at school," he remarked casually.

"I'm ditching calculus," she admitted. "I felt like coming here. What about you? Aren't you supposed to be at school?"

"I wasn't in the mood." He pointed to the top of the ramp. "You mind if I jam with you?"

Angie shook her head. "Go 'head."

She watched as Buzz went up to the lip of the ramp and then took off, his legs sure and strong on his skateboard, the smile on his face unmistakable. "Nice moves," she congratulated him as he came down. "You'll have to show me the stalefishgrab some time."

"Sure. What's wrong with now?"

"Nothing." She picked up her board and followed him.

"It's pretty easy," Buzz assured her. "All you have to do is use your rear hand to grab the board behind you. The trick is to bring your hand behind your rear leg."

Angie did as he said. She managed to grab

the board, but her landing was a little awkward.

"Almost," Buzz encouraged her. "You wanna try it again?"

Angie shook her head. "I need a rest." She plopped down on the grass and leaned back on her elbows, watching as Buzz took a few more jumps.

"You looked nice up there," she told him a while later, as he sat down beside her.

"Thanks . . . for everything, I mean."

"I thought we weren't mentioning that ever again," Angie reminded him.

"I know, but I just want you to know that I appreciate you coming to get me like that. I don't think there's anyone else who'd do that for me. I'll never forget it, Angie. If I'd had to call my old man . . ."

"Shhh . . . ," Angie said gently. She looked down at the scar on Buzz's arm—the one where his father had stubbed out a cigarette in a drunken rage. "Don't even think about it."

"I can't help thinking about it," Buzz said, his voice suddenly taking on a serious, longing tone he rarely shared with anyone. "It meant a lot."

"That's what friends are for," Angie replied sincerely.

"Is that all we are, Ange? Just friends?" He leaned closer to her, his eyes searching for something more. "I know better than that. And I think you do too."

"Come on, Buzz . . . ," Angie began. But she stopped herself. Why was she fighting Buzz so hard? He obviously cared about her. And more importantly, she knew all about him. He had no secrets hiding in his closet, ready to jump out and slap her across the face. Besides, Angie really needed someone to hold her right now.

She leaned toward him and placed her mouth on his. The reaction was instantaneous. After all, Buzz had been waiting for this for a long time. All the hunger he'd felt for her poured out of him in a powerful rush. He opened his mouth wider and plunged his tongue hungrily into her mouth, pulling her closer to him and running his fingers through her hair.

Angie didn't fight him. Instead she returned his kisses, struggling to make herself believe that this was the right thing to do. Buzz took his cues from her, and with each kiss he clung tighter to her, until they were lying on the ground with his body pressed hard on top of hers. She could hear him breathing heavily as he ran his lips down her cheek and into the small of her neck. All the while, his hands were moving quickly, rubbing up and down her body, moving beneath her T-shirt.

"Whoa, slow down," Angie whispered, gently moving his hands away.

"What?" Buzz asked, surprised. "Come on, Angie, you know you want this as much as I do."

Did she? Angie didn't know what she wanted. She wasn't really sure why she was lying here at this moment with Buzz. Was it because she really liked him? Was she just trying to get back at Carter Morgan? Or was it just possible that she was making out with Buzz because she had no one else and she was tired of being alone?

It was probably a little bit of all of three. Angie couldn't be certain. In fact, the only thing Angie knew for sure was that until she figured things out, having sex with Buzz could only lead to more problems for her.

"We can't do this right now," she told him, sitting up slowly and adjusting her shirt.

"Why not? It's just us. There's no one around for miles."

Angie shook her head. "It's not that. I'm just not sure. I'm not ready to . . ."

Buzz sighed and sat up beside her. "Okay, Angie. Whatever you want."

Angie reached over and kissed him gratefully on the cheek. "I just need some time."

"It's all right," Buzz assured her. He shrugged. "We were meant for each other, Angie. There's no hurry. We have our whole lives."

Angie turned away suddenly so he couldn't see the single tear that had just run down her cheek.

The first thing Angie noticed when she returned to school in time for third period was the big red love bite on her neck. "Damn it, Buzz," she cursed as she examined the bruise in the mirror that hung inside her locker.

Quickly she scrambled through her locker, searching for something she could use to cover the mark. She tore through the various items she'd stockpiled there in the days since school had begun—a collection of black T-shirts, some extra earrings, black nail polish, eyeliner. Finally she came upon a thick, leather dog collar with silver studs on it. Actually, the collar wasn't even hers. LeeAnn had stashed it in Angie's locker after stealing it from some store. At the time, Angie had been pissed off that LeeAnn was using her locker to stash her hot stuff, but right now, the choker would come in very handy. She wrapped it around her neck, snapped it tight, and walked off to class.

10

That afternoon Angie snuck out the side door of the school, anxious to avoid Buzz, who she was pretty sure would be waiting for her outside the main door. She wasn't ready to deal with him just yet, mostly because she wasn't at all sure what she wanted.

She spent her whole walk to work thinking about the past twenty-four hours. Everything had turned upside down, like a bad flip off the lip of a ramp. One minute she was out on a real date with a guy who seemed to be sent straight from heaven. But he turned out to be a total jerk. The next thing she knew she was making out with Buzz McGrath, who could come off as a real jerk, but deep down was actually a pretty nice guy.

As Angie turned the corner and walked into

the parking lot, she silently prayed that Sk8 4Ever would be crowded all afternoon. She didn't want to have time to think. It was making her head ache.

But there was only one customer in the shop as Angie walked in. Surprisingly, that customer was her aunt Dodo.

"*Bonjour,* Angie," Dodo greeted her. "What an interesting necklace."

Angie's hand went immediately to her throat, remembering the hickey hidden beneath the dog collar. She really didn't feel like explaining that to Dodo and Cody.

"Thanks," she muttered quietly, then headed toward the back room to start painting decks.

"Where are you going?" Cody asked her.

"I thought I'd get going on those new boards. I had a great idea for a Hawaiian-themed pattern. Sort of bring the whole surfing/skateboarding thing together."

"Sounds cool," Cody agreed. "Don't you want to know why your aunt's here?"

Angie shrugged. "She's probably filling you in on the date from hell I had last night."

Cody shook his head. "Nope."

"I didn't say a word," Dodo vowed. "You know I would never betray your confidence."

Angie looked down at the ground, suddenly ashamed of her distrust. She knew Dodo better than that. "Sorry," she said quietly. She turned to Cody. "He was one of the wormy ones."

Dodo looked at her niece curiously. *"Excusez-moi?"*

"Long story," Cody told her.

"Long, *corny* story," Angie said, smiling slightly for the first time all day.

"How bad?" Cody asked.

"The wormiest. A big fat liar."

"What'd he lie about?"

"Probably everything," Angie replied with disgust. "Starting with his name. *Chad Montgomery?* How could I have believed that one? You guys were right. It was something out of a soap opera."

"So what was the real name? Something goofy like Grover or Sidney?"

Angie shook her head. "Worse. Much worse. Try this on for size: Carter Morgan III."

Cody's eye twitched slightly. "*The* Carter Morgan III?"

"The terry-cloth heir himself."

Cody's eyes drifted toward Angie's neck. "Did he do anything to you? Hurt you? Attack you? Is that why you're wearing that collar?"

Angie shook her head vehemently. "No, that's . . ." She stopped herself. No point telling them about her and Buzz yet. Not until she was sure there was anything to tell. "It's just a fashion statement. He was a perfect gentleman. We had a great time—till I found out who he was. And get this—he didn't even have the guts to tell me himself. I had to find out from some of his loser friends."

"So you're dumping him for his name?" Cody asked.

"Uh, *duh,*" Angie spat back. "Why else?"

Cody shrugged. "Well, he was probably afraid to tell you who he was."

"That's exactly what I told her," Dodo agreed.

"Afraid?" Angie asked. "Carter Morgan III afraid of me? What could I do?"

"How about react exactly the way you're doing right now? You're being pretty petty, blaming someone for his name."

"It's more than his name. It's his whole family. They're a bunch of rich, nasty freaka-zoids. And I'll bet this wormy apple isn't falling far from the tree. They never do."

"That's why you're so much like your parents, right?" Cody asked her.

Angie grimaced. "Low blow," she grumbled. Cody was well aware of how hard she was fighting to be as unlike her parents as possible.

"Exactly," Cody said. "Some kids do break out of the nest, you know, kiddo."

Angie frowned. "I don't want to talk about this anymore," she grumbled.

"Okay," Dodo interrupted. "Let's talk about me. Don't you want to know why I'm here?"

"Why?"

"I'm going to take skateboard lessons from Cody!" Dodo was nearly bursting with excitement.

Whoa! Angie did a quick calculation in her head. Dodo had to be at least forty. She was going to take up skateboarding now? Angie couldn't imagine Dodo ollieing in one of her long flowing skirts at the ramp. "But, Aunt Dodo, it's kind of dangerous. If you fall from the ramp . . ."

"Relax, kiddo." Cody laughed. "I'm not going to have her doing three-sixties off a ramp. Let's face it, pavement gets harder the older you get."

Dodo shot him a look. "Speak for yourself. I'm not getting older. I'm ageless."

"Whatever," Cody continued. "Anyway,

she's gonna learn to slalom." He laughed at Angie's expression. "Wipe that look of shock off your face. It's not like you hit forty and go right to the old-age home, you know. Your aunt can handle this."

"Oh, I'm sure," Angie said, relieved that Cody was teaching her aunt to slalom. It was less dangerous than freestyle jumping, but it was still a great feeling. The whole point of slaloming was speed. Sometimes, really experienced slalom skaters could go as fast as twenty-five miles per hour—but you never left the ground.

"I'd love to paint a board for you, Aunt Dodo," Angie said excitedly. She was kind of glad that her favorite aunt would be entering her world—well, sort of. Slalom was different than what she and the kids did at the ramp, but the emotions could be the same. "It'll take me a few days, though. Can you wait till then?"

"Actually, we're going to start today," Cody explained. "I'm loaning her a board for a while."

Angie looked at him, surprised. Cody never loaned out boards. "You must really rate, Aunt Dodo," she complimented her aunt.

"Of course I do," Dodo replied. "So let's get started, Cody. Where's that helmet I just paid for?"

"It's right here . . ." Before Cody could fetch Dodo's new helmet, the bells jingled above the door.

There was dead silence as Cody, Dodo, and Angie all looked over just in time to see Carter Morgan III entering the store.

"Hi," Carter said, fully aware of the shock wave he'd sent through the shop.

"It's nice to see you again," Dodo said sweetly. "And so soon."

"You too," Carter replied. "How are you, Cody?"

"Fine," the shop owner replied. "And you?"

Angie couldn't believe her ears. What was with all the small talk? Was she the only one who couldn't believe the balls this jerk had, coming in here after what he'd done? "Didn't you get the message loud and clear last night?" Angie barked out. "I don't want to see you ever again. You stay on your side of the tracks, and I'll stay on mine."

"I'm not here to see you," Carter replied calmly.

"Then what are you here for?" she demanded.

"A skateboard. That's what you sell here, isn't it?"

Angie opened her mouth to speak, but Cody leaped in front of her. "It sure is," he told Carter. "Who are you buying it for?"

"Myself."

"Oh, give me a break," Angie moaned. "You don't skateboard."

"Not yet I don't. But I want to learn. It says on the sign in the window that I can arrange for lessons here as well. So I'd like to get the equipment and a board. I'd also like to sign up for some lessons."

"You came to the right place," Cody said excitedly.

Angie could see he was calculating big bucks in his head. Suddenly, she was very disappointed in her boss. She'd always thought he was one of the good ones. Now he was selling a board to a jerk like Carter just for the cash? "Cody, can I speak to you in the back?" she requested through gritted teeth.

"Excuse us a moment," Cody said as he followed Angie into the back office. "Look around."

"What are you doing?" Angie demanded once they were alone.

"Selling skateboard equipment."

"I know that," Angie huffed. "But to him?"

"What's wrong? Is his money counterfeit or something?"

"Very funny."

"I'm serious. Look, do you want that skatepark or not? I know *I* do."

"And you're willing to deal with the devil to get it?"

"What? He's the devil now?"

"You know what I mean."

"All I know is, if you want to work here, you'll have to treat all the customers with the same amount of respect," Cody told her, suddenly sounding very official.

Angie got the message. "Fine, whatever you want."

"That's what I want to hear. Now go pile up some pads and guards for him to wear. He'll need a helmet, too."

"He's got a motorcycle helmet," Angie informed him.

"Nah. Too big, too heavy. He needs one of the lighter ones that we sell," Cody said. "I'm going to dig through these boards and find him a good starter. Where's that one you painted of the spider with the fly in its web?"

Angie's eyes flew open. "You're going to sell him one of *my* boards?"

161

"I'm gonna try. They're our high ticket items."

In less than half an hour, Cody had managed to put more than three hundred dollars of Morgan money into his cash register. And that didn't even include what he was going to charge Carter for the hour-long lessons he wanted to take.

"Okay, so do you give the lessons?" Carter asked Cody. "I'd love to start today if I could."

"Well then, it's not me," Cody told him. "I'm going to be working with Dodo this afternoon." He turned toward Angie. "You'll have to work with the second string."

"I don't think anyone could ever call Angie 'second string,'" Carter said earnestly.

Dodo nodded appreciatively at the comment. "Damn straight," she agreed. "Angie's the best."

"That's why I could teach *you,* Aunt Dodo," Angie interrupted quickly. "That way Cody could work with Carter. He'd really get his money's worth learning from a champion."

Dodo shook her head. "No offense, *ma cherie,* but I don't think a kid like you could ever understand the limitations of this body . . .

young and perfect as it may seem," she joked, spinning around so her skirt blew up around her.

"Well, I can't work with Carter anyway, because someone has to watch the shop." Angie smiled triumphantly, certain she'd won this battle.

"No, it's okay," Cody said. "It's almost five o'clock already. I can close an hour and a half early. No one's coming in now."

Angie slumped down, defeated.

"You should probably go to the skatepark in Harrison," Cody said. "It's got a good beginner ramp."

"Harrison?" Angie asked. "How are we supposed to get there?"

"Carter has his car with him, doesn't he?"

"Actually, I have my motorcyle, but . . ."

"That'll do just fine," Coby assured him. He grabbed the black helmet from behind the counter. "Here Ange, you'll need this."

Angie rolled her eyes and took the helmet from him. "I'll just go get my board," she moaned.

Cody followed her. "Angie," he whispered. "Remember, this is business. Don't let your feelings enter into it. And whatever you do, don't let him get injured. That's all I need."

163

"Aren't you going to make him sign a release first?" Angie asked.

"Yeah," Cody agreed. "I'm not afraid of a lawsuit or anything. It's just that I don't need a *Morgan* getting hurt, okay?"

Angie nodded. "Don't worry boss, I won't let anything happen to Richie Rich out there. I swear."

11

A few minutes later, Angie found herself back on Carter's motorcyle, barrelling down the highway on the way to the skatepark. Once again she had her body wrapped around his. The sweet smell of his cologne wafted around her, bringing with it a swarm of memories that she wasn't interested in having return. But returning they were, and it was hard to fight the feelings that came with them. It was as though her mind and her body had two different agendas. Her mind wanted to stay as far from him as possible, but her body felt a need to cling to him that she couldn't comprehend. It was all so confusing. She was very relieved when they reached the Harrison skatepark.

"Okay, I think we should start with the basics first," Angie said, helping him put on his pads. "On flat ground. Then I can move you up to the low ramp." She pointed to an area of the park that was mostly populated with elementary-school kids.

"Just me and the rugrats, huh?" Carter joked.

Angie shrugged. "I mean, we could start you up there, but . . ." She pointed to an expert ramp in the distance.

"No, that's okay," Carter gulped. "We'll do it your way."

Angie spent the next few minutes showing Carter the parts of the board, demonstrating which was the front and which was the back, and letting him get used to moving with both legs planted firmly on the deck of the board. Once he was able to move a good distance without wobbling too much, Angie decided it was time to move to the small ramp.

"Okay, you go up to the lip, and I'll wait down here for you. Don't try anything fancy. Just stick with what we've been doing." She looked down at his wrist. The setting sun was reflecting off of his gold watch. "You'd better let me hold on to that," she said. "You don't want to smash it or—"

"Smash?" Carter suddenly sounded nervous.

"Well, I didn't mean you would smash into anything, just that—" Angie thought for a second, trying to rephrase so he wouldn't be scared off the ramp. "It's just that it falls off sometimes, right? And you wouldn't want it to lose it in midair."

"True." He slipped the watch from his wrist and handed it to her. Then he took a deep breath and started toward the top. When he reached the lip, he looked down at Angie. She wasn't very far away—maybe a few feet—but she could have been miles away as far as he was concerned.

"What if I fall off the board?" he shouted down to her.

"You won't," she called back to him.

"But if I . . ."

"I'm right here to catch you," Angie assured him.

"I don't know, Angie, I'm pretty heavy and . . ."

"I'll catch you." She was firmer this time.

"Come on mister, move it," a nine-year-old boy shouted. "I'm waiting here."

"Yeah, *mister,* move it," Angie joked.

"You'd better catch me," Carter warned. "I don't want to fall on my face and wind up looking like a Picasso or something."

Angie laughed heartily, imagining Carter with his eyes squished to the side of his face or his nose pointing the wrong way, like the subjects of some of Pablo Picasso's more abstract paintings. It was a perfect analogy.

"I'll catch you. Trust me."

"Okay," Carter shouted. "Here goes nothing." Taking in a big gulp of air, he forced himself to move down the ramp.

Angie watched as he moved. She saw a smile emerge on his face as the feeling took over. She recognized the expression immediately. She'd had the same expression of ultimate joy the first time she'd taken a ramp. *Carter had felt the magic.*

"Whoa," Angie shouted as Carter skated into her arms. She held him tight to stop him from stumbling as he hit the bottom of the ramp. "Nice one."

"That was so cool," Carter exclaimed. "Amazing."

"See, I told you you could trust me," Angie said, letting him go.

"That's more than you can say for me, right?" Carter sighed, searching her green eyes for some sign of forgiveness.

"Whatever," Angie turned from his gaze. "You want to try it again?"

"Okay," Carter said. He headed back to the top of the ramp. She watched as he rode down again, more sure of himself this time.

"It gets easier every time you do it," Angie said as he reached the bottom of the ramp. "More fun, too." She looked at his watch, which she'd fastened to her wrist. "Our time's about up, though." She slipped his watch from her wrist and gave it back to him.

"Okay. You wanna get a soda or something before we head back?"

Angie was reluctant. But she remembered Cody's warning about treating Carter like any other client, and she didn't want to insult him or anything. "All right. But quickly. I've got to get back."

They ordered two Cokes at the snack bar, found a small table that didn't have too much ketchup smeared on it, and sat down.

"So I guess I owe you an apology," Carter said in a low, thoughtful voice.

"You *guess*?" Angie began angrily, forgetting her promise to Cody.

"Look, I'm sorry, okay?" Carter apologized. "Really. I didn't start out wanting to lie to you. It's just that when I overheard your friends talking about my grandfather and how he was

169

trying to block their plans for a skatepark, well, I kinda got scared."

Angie thought about that for a moment. She couldn't really blame him there. If Buzz and the others had gotten wind of who he was, Carter could've been really hurt. "I guess my friends can seem kind of menacing," she agreed.

"Oh, I wasn't scared of them," Carter corrected her. "I can handle myself pretty well. I was scared you'd run out of there and I'd never get a chance to know you."

Angie didn't know what to say to that. It was probably true, actually. And at the moment, it didn't seem like something she was particularly proud of. "Look, forget it," she said. "It's all water under the bridge."

"I'm forgiven?"

"Sure," Angie said. "Why not? If I'm going to teach you to skateboard, we're going to have to get along."

His face fell. "Oh right. The lessons."

"So, we're being totally honest now, right?" Angie asked him.

"Mmm-hmm."

"Then tell me. Did you really come to the shop to learn to skateboard, or were you looking for me?"

"Both," Carter admitted.

"You wanted to learn to skate?"

"For a few days now."

What an odd answer. "Days?"

"Sure. Ever since I met you. I knew skateboarding was important to you, and I figured if I was going to become a part of your life, I'd have to understand why. This was a good way to do it."

Angie stared at him, surprised. No one she knew had ever cared enough to try and get inside her head like that. She gazed into his eyes and found herself smiling softly. Her body relaxed and she leaned slightly toward him as she felt herself surrendering to the feelings she'd begun to experience before—at Hamburger Heaven, on his motorcycle, and in Chez Français. At that moment she wanted nothing more than to just melt into his arms and tell him it didn't matter what his name was, or who his grandfather was.

But it *did* matter. It mattered a lot. And Angie knew it. She had to stop this right now, before things went too far. Before someone wound up getting hurt. "We'd better get back," she said quietly, tossing her empty Coke cup into a nearby trash can.

XXX

Carter dropped Angie off in the parking lot of Sk8 4Ever a few minutes before six. The light was on in the shop. Cody was obviously back from his lesson with Dodo.

"If you want, I can give you a ride home. I'll wait for you to get your stuff."

"That's okay. I can walk. I have a few things to do here anyway."

As she undid the chin strap of her helmet, her hand brushed against LeeAnn's dog collar, shifting it slightly up her neck and exposing the hickey Buzz had left there that morning.

"Okay, well, I'll see you Monday at five for my next lesson, right?" he said, sounding more businesslike now.

"You got it," Angie agreed, not understanding the sudden change in his tone. "Practice if you can. Maybe in your driveway." She stopped herself, considering how Old Man Morgan would feel about that. "Or somewhere."

Carter nodded, turned on the engine, and rode off without a word.

Angie watched him go, confused at his behavior. He'd completely shut down, just like that. *Out of nowhere.* Not that she could blame him. They could never be anything more than

172

acquaintances. Circumstances just wouldn't allow it. He'd obviously gotten her message, and agreed. She'd won the battle.

So how come she felt so lousy about it?

"How'd it go? Cody asked as she walked into the store. He eyed her neck and laughed. "Pretty well, I see. Did you two manage to get any skateboarding in?"

"Of course we did. What else . . ." Suddenly Angie caught a glimpse of her reflection in the metal of the cash register. The hickey on her neck jumped out at her, eclipsing just about everything else. "Oh man," she moaned, hurrying to cover it. So that was why Carter had just taken off like that. "This isn't what you think," Angie assured Cody.

"Whatever you say, kiddo. As long as he learns to skate."

"He will," Angie vowed. "He and I are strictly business."

"Hey Angie," Buzz's voice rang out as he entered the shop. "You about finished here?"

"Buzz!" Angie jumped. "What a surprise. I didn't expect you to come here tonight."

"I stopped by earlier, but no one was here."

"I was . . . uh . . . giving a lesson to a rich kid," Angie said quickly. "No big deal."

Buzz laughed. "So you got conned into that, didya? It wasn't that Britty, was it?"

"No. Someone else."

"It's getting pretty dark, and I didn't want you to have to go home by yourself," Buzz explained.

"I've always done it before. It's no biggie."

"Things were *different* before," Buzz said with a particularly proprietary air.

Cody sighed, suddenly realizing how wrong he'd been about the source of the mark on Angie's neck. But he said nothing. "Go ahead. I can close up here."

"You heard the man," Buzz said. "Come on. Maybe we can stop off by the lake, see if the submarine races have started yet."

"Real smooth, Buzz," she frowned. "Where'd you get that line from, your dad? I'll bet you use it on all the girls."

"There are no other girls," he told her as he bent down and kissed the nape of her neck.

Angie eventually convinced Buzz that she just wanted to go home. She was relieved when he finally laid off the idea of going to the lake, as she was anxious to avoid another heavy make-out session. But Buzz was determined to make that happen, no matter where they were. When they reached her front porch, Buzz leaned against the outer wall of her house and pulled her close to him. "You're gorgeous, you know that?" he said in a deep voice. "No one has ever turned me on the way you do, Ange. And no one has ever made me wait for so long either."

"Look, Buzz, I told you this morning. I'm not ready for that yet."

Buzz stepped away and took a deep breath. "I know you think I'm just another loser, Angie. That you'd be wasting your time with me. But I've got big plans. Do you know what I did when you went back to school today?"

Angie shook her head.

"I took the train to Pittsburgh and signed up for next spring's Regionals."

Angie stared at him, surprised. The regional skateboarding competitions were a big deal. Some of the best skaters in western Pennsylvania would be competing there—even a few professionals. Buzz would have to work his butt off to get to that level by April. That was only six months away. "Regionals? Wow. That's awesome, Buzz."

"Do you know why I did it?" he asked her earnestly. "For you, Ange. I wanted you to see that I was serious about getting us out of this place. The whole time I was signing up, I kept picturing how excited you'd be when I told you. I imagined what it would be like at the comps, with you in the stands rooting for me. I'm going to make you proud to be mine, Angie. You'll see."

Angie felt a cold shiver go up her spine. She pulled her black hoodie tighter against her and fiddled nervously with the cord that hung from the hood. She knew Buzz was trying to show her how much she meant to him. This was a sweet side of Buzz she'd never come across before. She felt a genuine tenderness toward him. But at the same time, he was scaring her. He was planning the rest of their lives. It was all too much too soon.

But looking at the hopeful expression on his face, she couldn't bear to talk to him about that now. He was so pleased and proud of himself. She couldn't ruin the moment. It would be too cruel. And so, when he leaned over to kiss her, she did nothing to stop it.

Buzz wasn't gone very long when Angie heard Aunt Dodo coming down the stairs from her apartment above the garage.

"You're not being fair to him," Dodo said as she walked over beside Angie and lit up an herbal cigarette. "Or to yourself."

"What are you talking about?" Angie asked with feigned innocence.

"Buzz McGrath. It'll never work out between the two of you. Better to end things now, before you completely break his heart."

"You don't know anything about me and Buzz," Angie retorted, angry that her aunt was butting into her business. Angry that she was probably right.

"I don't have to," Dodo told her gently. "I only know it isn't in the cards."

Great. Her aunt had been doing readings on her. *Just what I need right now.* "Your tarot cards don't know everything," Angie retorted.

"What the cards don't know, *you* do." Dodo touched her head and her heart. "You just have to accept it."

12

"**O**kay now this time, try not to use your hands," Angie called up to Carter. "You've almost got it." It was Monday evening, and they were back at the skatepark in Harrison. Angie was trying to teach Carter how to ollie. He had to master that basic jump before he could learn anything else.

"Here goes nothing," he called down to her as he leaped from the ramp—and floated through without using his hands at all.

She was genuinely impressed. Too bad Carter had gotten started so late. He could have been one hell of a skateboarder. Angie chuckled to herself at the thought of Carter as a skater boi like Buzz or Zack. She just couldn't imagine him in all black with a thick stud through his ear and a tight cap covering that unruly blond hair.

Still, he really did seem to love it. It was like there was a bad boy inside of him just dying to break free—and Angie was definitely willing to help him there. She really went for that whole bad-boy thing. Which was exactly what Buzz was counting on.

Buzz. Boy, would he be pissed off if he knew what Angie was doing right now. Sure, it was all business, but Buzz would never believe that. And now that he figured she was his girlfriend, he'd be willing to fight anyone who challenged him. It was amazing how he'd taken to acting around her since Thursday morning. On Friday, he'd shown up outside every one of her classes, just so he could walk her around the school. And all weekend, whenever she was at the ramp, he was all over her. Buzz was marking his territory, letting everyone know that he and Angie were together and that any challengers had better keep their distance.

"So, what'd you think?" Carter asked as he raced over to Angie.

She looked at him and smiled. His eyes were wide open and excited. His expression was adorable, like a little boy begging for approval.

"It was wicked awesome. Next time I'll teach you a couple of easy tricks. You're a natural!"

Carter's grin was overwhelming. "Thanks, Angie. Coming from you, well, that means everything."

"Not really," Angie said. "What matters is how *you* felt about your jump."

"It was incredible. That moment when you leave the ramp, just before you start coming down, man—there's nothing like it."

Angie knew exactly what he meant. It *was* the most incredible feeling. And it was impossible for someone who didn't own a skateboard to comprehend.

"So, um, you want to get a soda or something?" Carter asked her.

Angie shook her head. "It's starting to rain. I think we'd better head back."

"Good thing I brought the car this time," he agreed, pulling his keys from his jacket pocket.

Angie followed him to the silver Volkswagen and got in the passenger side. Carter sat down beside her and stared straight ahead. "So, um, who's this guy you're seeing?" he asked, trying to sound nonchalant but unable to look at her.

"Seeing?" Angie asked. "No one, really."

"Oh," Carter said quietly. "Guess it's none of my business. Sorry."

"No, it's okay. It's just that I'm not actually

seeing anybody. Not seriously, anyway."

"So nobody left that hickey on your neck last week?" Carter asked. He didn't sound angry or accusatory. Just sad and slightly vulnerable.

"Oh, that was just Buzz fooling around," she said. Then, realizing that she probably sounded like she'd been busy doing what his friends had accused her of, she added, "It's not what you think. He and I . . . well . . . we have a long history."

"Oh."

"Not *that* kind of history," she added quickly, not knowing quite what to say about Buzz. "I mean we've never . . . *I* haven't ever . . ."

"It's okay Angie," Carter said quietly. "You don't owe me any explanations."

"But I *want* to tell you," she said, the truth of the simple statement shocking even her. "Buzz and I, we've known each other so long, and everyone just sort of figures that some day we'll . . . and I guess he expects it too. But I don't want him . . ." She found herself getting more and more tongue-tied.

It was Carter who finally ended the conversation. He leaned over and kissed her gently.

Angie pulled back, shocked.

"I'm sorry," Carter apologized immediately. "It's just that I've wanted to do that all day. I've only kissed you at that hamburger place, but I've been playing it over and over again in my head. I can't seem to let go of it, and I guess I just wanted to see if that kiss was really as incredible as I remembered."

"And was it?"

Carter sighed. "You have no idea."

"Oh yeah," she corrected him. "I do." She leaned over and returned the kiss.

He wrapped an arm around her and drew her close to him. She rested her head against his chest and heard his heart beating. The quickness of the beat matched the excitement she felt in her own heart. The rhythms were simultaneous, and that seemed incredible. The fact that their hearts could beat as one like that, maybe it was some sort of sign that they were meant be together—despite all the obstacles. She looked up at him, letting her eyes do the talking for her.

He bent his head down and kissed her, this time with a little more certainty. She ran her hand through his soft blond hair and pulled him closer, wrapping herself in him as though he were a warm blanket that would keep her from all the cold in the world.

Angie was afraid to have Carter drop her off at Sk8 4Ever. Buzz had been hanging around there a lot, and she didn't want there to be any confrontation between the two of them. "Maybe you'd better just let me off here," she said as his car pulled up to the red light at the intersection just before the turnoff to the shop.

"Why?"

"Look, you and I . . . well . . . people wouldn't understand."

"People?"

Angie sighed. She couldn't hide anything from him. She barely knew him, and yet he could read her like a book. "Zack, LeeAnn, Buzz . . . you know."

"Oh, *Buzz*," Carter repeated.

"No. Buzz isn't the problem. There's nothing there. There never could be." It was true. There could never be anything between her and Buzz, or her and anyone else for that matter, because now and forever it would be Carter. "It's just that they could make a lot of trouble for you . . . and for me."

He looked at her doubtfully.

"Your friends wouldn't be too happy about seeing us together either," Angie reminded him.

Carter couldn't argue with her logic. "So what do we do now?" he asked. "I can't stay away from you, Angie."

She couldn't stay away from him either. "All I'm saying, you and I have to be careful. Maybe find our own turf. Someplace where we don't know a soul."

"New Charity," Carter said quickly.

"Excuse me?"

"New Charity. It's a little town up in the mountains. I only know about it because it's on the way to our summer house. There's no chance we'd run into anyone up there."

His summer house. Angie took a deep breath. Carter's life was so different from hers. The little trackhouse she shared with her parents was their summer, winter, fall, and spring house too.

"It's a tiny town. No one will bother us there. But it's almost two hours away. Is there any way you can get some time off this weekend?"

"I have Sundays off," Angie said. "But I was going to use the time to finish up my portfolio. I've gotta choose the fifteen slides that best show off my talent."

"Oh." Carter sounded disappointed. "That's really important. We can go some other time."

But Angie didn't want to go some other time. She wanted to be with him as soon—and as often—as possible. "Maybe I could bring the slides, and we could go through them together. Unless—I mean, you don't have to—"

Carter's eyes lit up excitedly. "I'd love to help you, Angie. I've never seen any of your artwork, unless you count the bottom of my board."

"It's different than that," she admitted.

He reached over, about to kiss her again, but the sound of beeping horns stopped him. The traffic light had turned green. Quickly, he signalled, drove over to the side of the road, and hit the brake.

This time, nothing could stop his lips from meeting hers.

Sure enough, Buzz was waiting for her at Sk8 4Ever when she walked up to the store. He was busy joking with Cody over by the register.

"How'd the lesson go?" Cody asked her as she handed him the extra helmet he'd loaned her to use at the skatepark. The park didn't let anyone skateboard without one.

"Oh man, you had to use headgear?" Buzz

laughed. "Cody, you're cruel. Bad enough you've got her teaching rich brats to board, now you've got her looking like a geek to do it. Angie, I'd better win a big comp quick, so I can take you away from all this."

Angie looked at the floor uncomfortably. She knew for certain now that there was no way she and Buzz were ever going to be anything more than friends. She just didn't know how she was going to tell him.

"I don't mind wearing a helmet," Angie said quietly. "It's good to teach new skateboarders to be safe."

Buzz shrugged. "Whatever. Anyhow, you ready to go? Zack, LeeAnn, Gina, and George are waiting for us at Hamburger Heaven."

"Hamburger Heaven?"

"Yeah, between us all we probably have enough for a couple of burgers and some baskets of fries. LeeAnn's dad passed out last night after he came home from McSorleys. She swiped some cash from his wallet."

Angie looked pleadingly at Cody. By some miracle he seemed to read her mind. "Sorry Buzz, I need Angie here tonight. Inventory," he explained.

"Oh." The disappointment was unmistakable

in Buzz's tone. "I guess I could stay and help . . ."

Angie smiled at him. "Don't be silly, Buzz. It's cool. I don't want you all bummed out because of me. Go have a good time. Say hi to everyone for me."

"Okay," Buzz agreed. "You're the best." He reached for her and kissed her hard, shoving his tongue deep into her mouth. He tasted rough and smoky, and Angie had to resist the urge to spit his tongue from her mouth. She was more than relieved when he finally released her from his grip and jauntily strutted out of the shop.

"Well, that was some display," Cody teased as Buzz left the store.

Angie blushed furiously. "I'm sorry," she apologized. "He didn't mean anything by it."

"Oh, he meant something," Cody corrected her. "You just didn't feel anything."

"You could tell?" Angie asked. She worried for a moment that perhaps Buzz had picked up on that as well. But she dismissed that idea just as quickly. Buzz was pretty dense when it came to registering unspoken signals.

"I noticed your expression when you saw that Buzz was here. It was like he'd popped your balloon or something." He watched her expression. "So you and Carter have figured things out, I guess."

"How'd you know?" Angie asked, wondering if her newfound love showed on her face.

"Your aunt Dodo. She predicted it. We were out working on her slalom techniques, and all of a sudden she said, 'They're going to need our help. The two of them won't have an easy time of it.' Somehow I knew she didn't mean you and Buzz."

"No, she didn't," Angie admitted.

"Your aunt's pretty amazing," Cody continued. "The way she just knows things, things other people never see."

Angie eyed her boss's face. "Sounds like someone's got a bit of a crush," she teased.

"I don't know what you're talking about," Cody replied coyly, turning away from her. "You count up the receipts from the register. I've got a few things to do in the back."

13

Angie woke up early Sunday morning and dressed in complete silence, anxious not to wake her parents. She didn't want to have to answer any questions. Not this morning.

A whole day alone with Carter! The idea both thrilled and petrified her. They hadn't spent more than a few hours at a time in each other's company. Now they were going to spend a full day together—and at least four hours of it stuck in a car. This day could be amazing . . . but it could also be a complete disaster.

She grabbed her backpack and her board and snuck out of the house and into the quiet morning. Her block was like a tired movie set—quiet facades of houses with not a human in sight. The silence was amazing. It was as though she were the only person for miles.

But the solitude didn't last long. A moment later, Angie smelled the pungent odor of her aunt Dodo's herbal cigarettes coming from the stairway that led to her apartment.

"You're up early," Dodo said as she walked around the corner to greet Angie.

"I, um . . . I have some stuff I have to do."

"Give Carter my best."

Angie blushed prettily. "How'd you . . . oh, never mind." There was no use asking Dodo how she knew anything. She just did.

"Where are you two off to?" Dodo asked her, smiling her approval of the union.

"Some small town up in the mountains—just for the day. We're going to look at my slides and have some lunch. That's all, honest." She patted her backpack where the slides were currently hidden.

Dodo grinned. "Don't worry. I'm not asking any questions. You're a big girl. You can make your own decisions."

Angie looked at her aunt gratefully. It was wonderful to have someone like her around. It actually felt good to share her secret with a person she could trust not to judge her. She was glad Dodo had been awake so early on a Sunday morning.

Come to think of it, that was extremely out of character for Dodo. She usually kept more vampirelike hours. "Why'd you get up so early?" Angie asked her suddenly.

Dodo gave her a secretive smile. "Actually, I'm just coming in."

Angie's eyes burst open. "You've been out all night?" she asked, amazed. "Where?"

Dodo laughed and turned toward her apartment. "You're not the only one with secrets, *ma cherie.*"

Carter was waiting in his car in the parking lot just outside Opal's Art Supply when Angie rolled in on her board about half an hour later. They'd decided to meet at the store because it was one place neither of their crowds would ever stop by. That made it a special, private place— one with a meaning only they could understand.

Angie bit her lip and tried not to laugh as she got in on the passenger side and looked over at Carter. He'd obviously shaved for her—and nicked himself in at least three places.

"Hi there," Angie said, giving him a little peck on the cheek. "Ooh, your skin's so smooth," she added, figuring she might as well acknowledge the effort.

A quick red tone took over his cheeks. "Thanks," he said with gruff embarrassment. "I . . . um, I sort of needed a shave."

"It looks nice."

Carter pointed toward the cup holder between them. "I got you a coffee. I didn't know how you took it, so I got you brown sugar, white sugar, Sweet 'n Low, and cream. I hope you don't use soy milk, because they didn't have any of that."

"I just take it black," Angie told him.

"I didn't even consider that," Carter admitted. "But I know it now. Now sweetener, no cream. It's just one more fact to add to my collection, right behind your passion for burgers and fries."

Angie sat back in the seat and smiled contentedly. The image of Carter stashing away little bits of information about her likes and dislikes was especially pleasing to her. Suddenly it struck her that she knew very little about him. Maybe it was time she started her own collection of facts.

"How do you drink *your* coffee?" she asked him.

"Just a little milk or cream," he said as he started the engine and began to drive.

"And how about eggs?" she continued.

"Eggs?"

"Yeah, how do you like your eggs?"

He glanced over at her. "Why do you want to know that?"

She shrugged. "Just curious, I guess. I read in some magazine that you don't really know a guy until you know how he likes his eggs."

"You read those kinds of magazines?" he asked, seemingly surprised.

"Sure. What'd you think? I only subscribed to skateboard mags or something?"

Carter laughed. "Scrambled. A little on the well-done side. I don't like that runny stuff."

"I'll remember that," she said. "How about your favorite color?"

"Orange. The brighter the better." He paused for a moment, then smiled confidently. "I'll bet I know yours. Black, right?"

"Wrong." Angie shook her head. "My favorite color is blue. All shades—navy, robin's egg, sky, even baby blue. I love all the variations. And there's something about blue being a primary color that makes it so vital to me."

Carter seemed surprised. "Blue, huh? That's not what I would've thought at all. What other surprises are you keeping?"

Angie took a sip of her coffee and settled

back in her seat. "That's for me to know and you to find out."

The drive to New Charity sped by. There was so much they wanted—*needed*—to know about each other. Every little detail seemed to be of the utmost importance. No fact seemed too small or trivial to bring up.

Finally Carter pulled over onto a tiny street and parked his car beside a small flowing stream. "Well, this is it," he said as he turned off the engine.

Angie looked around. There didn't seem to be anyone, or anything, around. Just the stream, a grassy knoll, and some trees. "Where's the town?" she asked him.

"Around the corner. It's not actually a whole town. It's sort of one block with a diner, a general store, a post office, and a tiny library. Do you want to see it?"

"Sure." Angie picked up her backpack and got out of the car. "Whoa, it's cold out," she said, pulling her black hoodie tighter around her.

"It gets cold early up here in the mountains. November up here's like January back in Torren. I should've warned you." He took off his thick brown suede jacket. "Here, put this on."

"But you'll freeze."

"It's not that far. Come on, put it on. I don't want you getting sick." He wrapped the coat around her shoulders.

She snuggled up in the warm coat and looked at him gratefully. He smiled down at her, his eyes blazing with pleasure at having been able to take care of her.

"Come on, let's hurry," she said, pulling him toward the single block that was the town of New Charity.

The diner was packed when Angie and Carter arrived, but they managed to find a booth for two in the back of the restaurant. Carter waited for Angie to settle into her seat before he took his jacket back. Then he started off toward the door.

"Where are you going?" she asked him.

"Just something I need to do," he replied. "I'll be back in a few minutes. Order for me, willya?"

"What do you want?"

Carter grinned. "It's still brunch, right? I'll have some eggs and coffee. You know how I like them."

He returned a few minutes later with a huge plastic bag. He handed it to her nervously. "This is for you."

195

Angie looked up, surprised. "What's that?"

"It's for you. Go ahead, open it."

Angie reached out and took the bag. She opened it quickly, tearing at it like a kid at Christmas. "Oh, my," she said when she released the gift from the bag. It was the brightest blue ski jacket she'd ever seen in her life. She wasn't quite sure how to react.

"You don't like it," he said, trying not to sound as disappointed as he felt.

"No, it's not that," she said. "I'm just surprised."

Carter sat down in his seat and took a sip of his coffee. "I saw it in the window of the general store as we passed by. I just got it for you now. You didn't have a warm coat and I sort of planned a special surprise for after lunch, and it's outside . . ."

"*Another* surprise?"

"You'll like this one better," he assured her.

"No way. I love this. I don't have anything this color." She slipped the jacket over her arms.

"Wow," he said softly.

"What?"

"Your eyes. They look even greener now. You should wear blue more often."

Angie snuggled into the coat. "I'm going to wear this all the time."

"How're your friends going to take that?" he asked her.

Angie grew quiet. It was the first time either of them had mentioned their respective groups of friends all day. It was sort of an uncomfortable subject. But at that moment, Angie said the truest words she would ever say. "I don't care."

"Here ya go, kids," the waitress said as she placed Carter's scrambled eggs and Angie's burger and fries on the table. "Enjoy."

The food wasn't anything special, but for Angie it was the most enjoyable meal she'd ever had. Afterward, they looked at the slides of her work, and he gave her feedback on each picture. He wasn't afraid to say that there were some he liked better than others, and she was grateful for his honesty. It meant he was really, truly looking at her work, and not just glancing at it.

When they'd gone through all the slides, and Angie had chosen the fifteen strongest candidates for her portfolio, she felt a new confidence come over her. "I think these will work," she said excitedly. "I really do. Now if I could just get those financial aid papers from my folks . . ."

"They're still holding back?" Carter asked.

Angie nodded. "They really don't want me to go. It's been one hell of a battle. I have to get this out next Monday if I'm going to make the deadline. But that still gives me eight days to work on them."

"Even if they don't fill them out, Angie, I could ask my—"

Angie shook her head vehemently. "No way, Carter," she said. "I'll get them to do it."

Carter nodded, knowing by now that this was one issue that wasn't negotiable. He reached into his pocket and pulled out his wallet. "Okay if I pay the check?"

Angie nodded. "I'll let you do that. It'll make it a real date."

He threw the cash down on the table. "Now come on, because if I don't show you this surprise, I think I'm gonna bust a gut.

"We have to drive there," Carter explained as he headed toward the car. He used his remote-control keyring to unlock the doors.

Angie climbed into the passenger side and buckled her belt. "How far?" she asked.

"Just a few miles. We have to go a little away from the main part of town."

"It gets more rural than this?" Angie laughed.

"Not exactly," Carter replied mysteriously.

"Are we going somewhere in the woods? Hiking?"

"Nope."

"It's outside, right? We just ate, so it can't be a picnic. How about painting? Are we going to sketch the landscape or . . ."

"You can guess all you want. But I'm not telling."

Angie frowned. *Talk about busting a gut.* She couldn't wait to find out where he was taking her. "Drive faster!" she demanded.

Carter made a lefthand turn. The bumpy country road became wider and smoothly paved. A maze of buildings came into view. It looked remarkably like Morgan Mills.

"A mill?" Angie asked. "You brought me to a *mill*?"

"Uh-huh," Carter replied, fighting the smile that was forming on his lips. "It's Barson's Mill. The only one up here."

"Is this some sort of sick joke? Bring the millbrat to a mill?"

"Angie," Carter interrupted with mock indignation. "I can't believe you would think such a thing." He parked the car. "Come on. Let's go."

"I'm not getting out of this car."

"But you have to." He reached into the backseat where she had stashed her board. "I have something to show you."

Reluctantly, Angie did as she was told.

"Come on," Carter pleaded eagerly, pulling her by the arm toward one of the buildings. Finally, when they'd reached their destination, he grinned with absolute joy and waved his arm in the direction of the empty loading dock behind the mill. It had a ramp that was paved smooth, and it was at just the perfect angle for skateboarding. "Check it out. This place belongs to Louis Barson, a friend of my grandfather's. I've been here plenty of times and I happen to know the mill's closed on Sunday. It's all ours. No bratty kids rushing us or getting in the way."

Angie jumped up and hugged him with excitement. "I'm so sorry I yelled at you," she apologized, kissing him hard on the mouth.

"Apology accepted," he replied, coming up for air. "Now, do you want to make out, or do you want to skateboard?"

"Do I have to choose?" she asked playfully.

"Come on," Carter pulled her toward the ramp. "I want to skate. You promised to show me a few things."

"Only if you promise to show me a few things later." Angie raised one eyebrow seductively.

"Oh, that's a given," he laughed, dragging her up to the loading dock.

The afternoon flew by quickly as Angie and Carter used the ramp to practice all sorts of jumps. She was careful not to do her best work for fear of hurting his male ego. She knew from experience that guys hated it when a girl outdid them too much.

But her experiences hadn't prepared her for a guy like Carter.

"I get the feeling you're holding back from me," he told her as she did a simple shoveit off the ramp. "I thought you were some sort of skateboard queen."

"You want me to really show you what I can do?" she asked, slightly dubious.

"Oh, yeah."

"Okay," Angie agreed. "Prepare to be amazed."

"I'm constantly amazed by you," he assured her.

She put down her board and strolled over to a collection of empty wooden cartons. She stacked the cartons on top of one another until she'd built a small tower. Then she headed up to the ramp and sped down, leaping off just in time to clear the cartons in a perfect nollie-shifty.

"Whoa!" Carter shouted with true amazement. He raced over and grabbed her around the waist, lifting her off the ground. "That was magnificent, like a ballet. Absolutely incredible." He kissed her.

"That was pretty incredible too," she whispered, pulling him down onto the ground.

The cement was cold and hard, but neither Angie nor Carter felt anything other than the magic of being so close together as their hands traced each other's bodies beneath the layers of sweaters and coats. It was as though there were no one else in the world beside the two of them.

But that wasn't true at all. In fact, there *was* someone else at the mill. He'd been watching the teens for quite a while and he didn't like what he'd seen one bit. He was horrified by the image of these kids skateboarding on the ramp—disrespecting his property. And he couldn't bear seeing them embracing. And so, as he watched Carter Morgan III carrying on with someone far below his stature, Louis

Barson pulled out his cell phone and called his old buddy, Carter Morgan, Sr.

"Carter, old boy," he said into the receiver. "I was making a quick inspection of my mill up here in New Charity. And I saw something I think you should know about. . . ."

To the other businessmen enjoying their late-afternoon cocktails at the club, it appeared that Carter Morgan had taken whatever news he'd just received on the phone quite calmly. The millionaire had long since mastered the art of keeping an outward visage of unruffled emotions. It was part of being a businessman.

But inside, the old man was seething. These skaters. They were taking over his town. Bad enough they walked the streets in their strange clothes, with earrings in places he hadn't even realized could be pierced. He hated the way their makeshift skate ramps brought down property values. But now they'd gone too far. Imagine them thinking they could make his grandson one of them. He wasn't going to let that happen. He'd seen what skateboarding could do to people. There was no way he was letting Carter's intelligence go to waste.

"Excuse me, gentlemen," he said as he rose

from his seat at the bar and moved to a secluded corner of the room. "I've got a deal in the making." Quickly he dialed the number of his most trusted realtor. "Bob?" he said. "Sorry to bother you so late on a Sunday, but I think it's time we made our move. Tell the owner of that lot beside the mill that I'm ready to buy."

14

"Just drop me off here," Angie told Carter as they drove back into Torren together.

"I'll take you home," Carter said.

Angie shook her head. "This is fine."

"Look, Angie, if it's about your house, or your neighborhood, I don't care. I—"

She leaned over in her seat and kissed him softly on the cheek. "It's not that. I don't have any secrets from you. It's just that there's something I need to do right near here."

"Do you want me to come with you?"

"Nope. This is something I've gotta do alone."

Carter knew better than to question her further. He pulled the car over to the side of the road. "So how about next Sunday? Do you want to go back up to New Charity?"

"Next Sunday is Thanksgiving weekend. Will you be able to get away?"

"Oh, yeah," Carter answered her. "By Sunday my family'll be ready to kill each other. They'll be relieved to have one less around."

"Sounds like my family. Dad's gonna spend Sunday the same way he spends every day of Thanksgiving weekend—glued to some football game. And Mom and Aunt Dodo'll be out shopping for pre-Christmas bargains."

"So I'll meet you at Opal's?"

"Sure. And don't forget you have a lesson with me tomorrow. It's prepaid so there's no backing out."

Carter laughed heartily. As if there were any chance of that happening.

It was only a few blocks from where Carter had left her to Hamburger Heaven, but in many ways it seemed the longest walk Angie had ever taken. She knew Buzz was going to be there. And she knew he was going to have a lot of questions. But she was going to have to face him sometime.

"Hey, Angie." Gina was the first of her friends to spot her as she entered the parking lot of Hamburger Heaven. She crossed the lot to greet Angie. "Where'd you get that jacket?"

"Oh, just some store," Angie told her as the two girls walked up toward the burger joint together. She noted Gina's expression. "Whatsamatter? You don't like it?"

"Well . . . it's just not your usual style is all," Gina said. "It's kind of preppie."

"Well, that's a first." Angie chuckled. "Someone calling me a preppie."

Gina giggled. "Yeah, like that would ever happen."

"Yo, Angie!" Buzz's familiar voice rang out as she got closer to the tables outside the restaurant. She spotted him right away. He was sitting on the hood of someone's car, drinking a beer. Zack, LeeAnn, and George were standing around him, laughing about something.

"Where you been today?" He leaped down from the car as she came closer and wrapped a strong arm around her. "And where'd you get this thing?" he asked, looking at her new jacket with disdain.

"It's really warm."

"But it's so *blue*." He said the word like it was some sort of joke.

"I *like* blue," Angie said indignantly.

"I've been lookin' for you all over," Buzz

said, changing the subject. "I even called your mom. She said you left before she got up."

"I was working on my portfolio." *It's the truth, after all.*

"Oh yeah, that thing," Buzz murmured dismissively. He reached into his jacket pocket and pulled out a bottle. "You want a brew?"

"No thanks. Um . . . Buzz . . . can I talk to you? Privately?"

"Ooh," Zack teased. "Private, huh? Don't worry about that, Ange. We won't look."

"Shut up," LeeAnn warned, poking him in the side. "We know you don't care where you get action, but maybe Angie does."

Buzz gave Zack and George a lascivious wink. "Whatever you say, baby. Your wish is my command." He pulled her closer and then walked off to a secluded area behind the restaurant, near the back door of the kitchen.

The smell of frying onions and raw meat permeated the area. Angie was tempted to move to someplace else to talk to Buzz, but she realized that no place was going to make this any better. She may as well do it here.

"Look, Buzz, we need to talk."

"Talk?" he asked. "What fun is that?" He leaned over close, and the beer-filled stink of his breath was added to the stench of the meat and onions. Angie felt slightly queasy.

"Buzz, this isn't easy for me."

"Don't worry, baby. I'll be gentle."

He was obviously drunk. That made things even harder. When Buzz was in this sort of state, there was no telling what his reaction would be. For a minute she considered talking to him tomorrow, or maybe even the day after, since Buzz with a hangover was worse than Buzz drunk.

No. She owed it to Carter—to herself—to do this now. "Buzz, this has gone too far already."

"Come on baby, you've already had the appetizer. Aren't you ready for the main course yet? I know *I'm* real hungry." He reached over and nibbled on her earlobe. Angie pulled away, repulsed. "We can go back to my house," Buzz continued, not noticing her reaction. "No one's there. Dad's out on a bender and Mom's at her cousin's, so we—"

"There is no *we,* Buzz. There never was. And there never will be." She blurted it out in a single breath, unable to keep her true feelings bottled up a moment longer.

He stared at her in silence for what seemed

an eternity. She watched his pale gray eyes open slowly, as the meaning of her words knocked the haze from them. "You're breaking up with me?"

"No," Angie said quickly.

"Then what?" Buzz demanded. "That's sure what it sounded like to me."

"I can't break up with you because we were never together. We made out a couple of times. That's all."

Buzz's face turned ugly, almost monster-like. "You damned slut!" he shouted.

Now it was Angie's turn to be shocked. "What?"

"You heard me. Boy, I was wrong about you, baby. *That coat.* You didn't buy that. You got that from someone." Angie watched his expression get more and more lucid as the pieces all came together for him. "It's that preppie scum. You haven't been teaching any rich brat to skate. And you weren't working on your damned portfolio today. You've been doing him, haven't you? You've been teasing me, and giving him the real deal!"

"No, Buzz. That's not true." Angie could feel the furor rising in her. Buzz had tried to lower her relationship with Carter to the basest form. He'd turned it into something animal-like. But what did she expect from someone like Buzz? It was all he knew. "I've been giving lessons, and I was looking at my slides. And as for all your other sordid accusations, just for the record, I haven't slept with anyone. *Ever.*" She didn't have to add that last bit, but for a strange reason she felt she owed him at least that.

"Sure," he spat back. "If you think I'm gonna believe that, you're nuts. What else could a guy like that want with someone like you? Sure, he treats you all fancy and buys you gifts." He spat at the sleeve of her coat. "But you watch. Once he's taken all he wants to, he'll dump you back on this side of town. Don't expect me to be wait-ing, Angie. You lost your shot."

Angie began to cry. It was irrational, she knew. She wasn't the one who'd been dumped. Still, something in Buzz's words struck a raw nerve. It was clear to her now that she'd been forced to choose between Carter and her friends. She would be a pariah to them now. There was no way Buzz was going to let her get away with this. He was going to make it clear that Angie wasn't one of them anymore. And the others would follow his directive. They always did.

A horrifying fear ran through her. What if Buzz was right? What if Carter really did just want to fool around with someone a little different? Someone a little more spicy than the white-bread girls in his neighborhood. What if he . . .

No! Angie wiped the thought from her head. *Not Carter.*

"Angie!" LeeAnn shouted. She had spotted her friend's tear-stained face as Angie raced back around the corner and through the parking lot. LeeAnn started to run to her, but stopped after seeing Buzz's expression.

"Buzz, man, what's happening?" Zack asked as Angie bolted past the crowd of skaters.

"I dumped her, man," Buzz said firmly.

"You what?" Zack couldn't believe his ears. "How could you do that, man?"

"She wouldn't give me what I wanted, and Buzz McGrath don't wait for nobody. I told her to go find that preppie dude or someone else who's gonna put up with that crap, and sent her packing."

Angie didn't stop to refute Buzz's version of things. She knew that he had to lie to keep his standing with his friends. She'd already hurt him enough. She couldn't take that away from him. Instead, she stormed out of the parking lot and turned toward home, leaving the skaters behind her.

15

Angie spent all of the school day on Monday avoiding Buzz and the others—ducking out through back doors, spending lunch on her own in the girls' room. It just seemed easier than seeing all of them together and no longer being a part of them. LeeAnn and Gina might have wanted to be friendly with her despite what had happened, but Angie knew that Buzz would never allow it. And what Buzz McGrath said, went.

Unfortunately, despite all her efforts, there was no avoiding Buzz forever. He was at Sk8 4Ever when she arrived at work. He, Zack, and George ignored her completely as she walked in the store. Even Cody just sat there behind the counter, his head buried in his hands. Luckily, Dodo was there to at least acknowledge her presence.

"Hello, Angie," she said with none of her characteristic enthusiasm.

"Who died?" Angie joked to the melancholy faces around her.

"Just our dreams," Buzz shot back. "Nothin' you'd care about."

"What?"

"Old Man Morgan bought the land next to the mill," George explained. "He's building an . . . an . . . what'd the sign say, Buzz?"

"It said 'Future Home of the Auxiliary Offices of Morgan Mills,'" Buzz recalled. "But don't tell *her* about it. Why would she care?"

"I care," Angie declared strongly. "I care plenty. But it doesn't make any sense. That lot's been for sale forever. Why would Carter Morgan suddenly decide to buy it now?"

"Because he can," Cody moaned. "I was so close. Just a few more thousand dollars and I could've had that lot."

"Don't give up, Cody," Dodo said gently. "There are other lots of places. Maybe in the next town or—"

"No!" Cody shouted. "Don't you get it? He'll stop me no matter where I go or what I do. He's never going to let this skatepark happen. He's a coldhearted SOB who gets his way

215

no matter what. There's no getting past him."

"But—," Zack began.

"There are no buts," Cody said, interrupting him fiercely. "Carter Morgan doesn't want skating in Torren or anywhere near it. And he's found a way to make sure it doesn't come here."

"No he hasn't," Buzz insisted. "He's only made sure the skatepark isn't built on the land next to his mill. But he hasn't stopped us from skateboarding. He can't do *that*."

"I know, Buzz," Cody said. "But I wanted a place where kids could have fun skating and not get hurt . . . the way I did."

The kids all sat there, silent. It was the first time Cody had ever told them anything about his past.

"You?" Zack finally asked.

Cody nodded. "It's still hard to believe. I rode some of the world's most radical waves and took on the biggest names in comps. And then I'm just fooling around on some stupid street ramp and *boom*. The next thing I know, the whole damn thing's on top of me. It was so stupid. I knew it wasn't a sturdy ramp, but I took the jump anyway. Smashed up my left leg, broke my jaw and my nose. The wood tore a massive hole in my cheek. And that was the end of everything."

Cody's story was finally out. Maybe it wasn't as exciting or romantic as the kids had once imagined, but it was fascinating. *And frightening.* The truth was, the same thing could happen to any of them. Anytime, anyplace.

Angie studied the jagged line on Cody's face. His story explained the scar on his face—and the tear in his soul. His love of competition had died on that ramp. A skater who couldn't skate was truly the saddest thing Angie could imagine.

"He's not getting away with this!" Buzz declared vehemently.

"Don't do anything stupid, Buzz," Cody warned. "Carter Morgan plays for keeps. He doesn't care who he knocks down along the way."

"Don't worry about me," Buzz replied. "I got it covered."

He stormed out of the shop, a young man with a mission. His foot soldiers, Zack and George, followed right behind him.

"I don't like the sound of that," Cody moaned as Buzz and the others left. "That's all I need, more people getting hurt. The whole point of the skatepark was to make it a safer sport for those guys."

"Listen, Cody, Carter's got a lesson today. Maybe if I ask him to talk to his grandfather, he could—"

"Don't do that," Cody warned in a powerful and foreboding tone. "Leave the kid out of this. Spare him. His grandfather'll make his life hell if he finds out he's been skating."

Dodo put a soft hand on Angie's shoulder. "You need to listen to him, *ma cherie*. He knows what he's talking about."

"But how?" Angie asked.

"It doesn't matter how or why," Dodo said softly. "You just have to respect his wishes." She led Angie to the door. "Maybe you should meet Carter outside today."

"Okay. Whatever you say, Aunt Dodo." She looked back at Cody. His face was ashen and his arms were shaking. "Is he going to be all right?"

"I'll take care of him," she promised her niece.

"What are you going to do?"

"The only thing I can do. I'm going to make him take me skateboarding."

Angie practically leaped into Carter's convertible as soon as he pulled into the parking lot. She leaned over and kissed him, grateful to see a friendly face after spending the day ditching kids who wanted to pretend they didn't know her. Carter returned her kiss, but there was something in his touch that troubled Angie.

"Is something wrong?" She was almost afraid to ask. Far too much had gone wrong today already.

"It's . . . nothing," Carter said slowly.

She knew he was lying. "No secrets, remember?"

Carter began to fidget nervously with the faulty clasp on his watch. "I don't want to lay my family issues on you. It's not fair."

"Hey, the Simms family practically defined the word 'dysfunctional.' There's nothing you can say I haven't been through. Maybe I can help."

Carter leaned back in his seat and stared out the window. "My grandfather knows . . . about us," he said slowly.

"Oh," Angie replied just as slowly. She bit her upper lip. "And let me guess, he's not too happy."

"It's not you, Ange, I swear. If he got to know you, I'm sure he'd—"

"He'd still be unhappy," Angie interrupted him. "You're grandfather isn't exactly hoping to have my picture on his mantel someday."

"It doesn't matter what he thinks, Angie. I'm not like him."

"I know," she said softly, brushing his bangs from his eyes.

"It was awful. You should've heard him." Carter's voice was breaking now. It was clear that he was frustrated with his grandfather's closed-minded attitude. "He was going on and on about ruined potential and skateboarding, and how he wasn't going to let it destroy another thing in this town. I've never seen him so angry. He threatened to cut me out of his will. Can you believe him? He always tries to use his money to get what he wants. You should see the way he uses it to pull my father's strings. Well, it's not going to work this time. I'm not my father."

Use his money to get what he wants. Slowly, it all came together in Angie's mind. "Oh, my God. It's all my fault!" she exclaimed.

Carter reached out and pulled her toward him. "No it's not," he swore to her. "My grandfather was a jerk long before I met you. He's been angry before. This is not your fault. Besides," he added, pulling her close to him and kissing her on the forehead, "what he doesn't know won't hurt us. We'll find ways to be together."

Angie shook her head. "No, you don't understand. Your grandfather just bought the lot of land next to the mill. The one Cody wanted to build the skatepark on. I couldn't figure out why Carter Morgan had suddenly shown an interest in some empty field, but now I get it. He was angry about me seeing you—and he's taking it out on all the skaters." Her voice was filled with shame. She felt disloyal to the people who had, up till now, been the most important to her. "Carter, we're hurting so many people. We have to think about them. Maybe we're being selfish by—"

He put a single finger against her lips. "Don't go there," he said softly. "I can't let you go now. You're a part of me."

Angie knew exactly what he meant. Leaving Carter now would be like amputating part of her heart. She would never survive it.

They sat there for a moment in the parking lot, holding each other close. Each lost in thought. Each grateful for the other's existence.

"We're going to have to be more careful now," Carter said finally. "We can't go to New Charity anymore. My grandfather's friend will be watching for us. Hell, the old man's probably got spies all over the place by now."

221

"Then where can we go?"

"I'll think of something," Carter promised her. "But I think we should probably stay away from the skatepark today. That's the first place he'll suspect." He frowned. "Damn. I was really loving learning to skateboard."

Angie thought for a moment. "You don't have to give that up," she said quickly.

"But Angie, he's going to be looking for us at the park."

"Who said we were going to the park? Start driving."

"Where are we going?"

"To an old ramp. Cody told me about it once when I was looking for a place to practice all by myself. Hardly anyone knows about it. It's kind of broken-down. I think some kid must have built it years ago and then just sort of abandoned it."

"Won't your friends be there?"

Ex-friends, Angie corrected him silently. "Nope. I don't think anyone knows about it except Cody. He said he just found it one day."

As Angie taught Carter how to casper on the old ramp, they had no idea that they were the topic of conversation in an office on the other side of town. Carter Morgan, Sr. had called a meeting of his newest employees—a group of three eighteen-year-old boys. They were all so-called friends of the old man's grandson.

"I suppose you've all met my grandson's latest paramour," Carter Morgan said as he surveyed the teens.

"We've seen her," the tallest one, Ted, replied dismissively. "A real piece of work."

"My thoughts exactly," Carter Morgan agreed. "As you can imagine, I don't approve."

"Neither do we, sir. She's definitely NOKD," Ted told him.

"NOKD?"

"Not our kind, dear," Ted translated. "It's one of my mother's favorite sayings."

"Well, it's definitely correct in this case. And while I've asked my nephew to reconsider his relationship with this young *lady*,"—the old man said the last word sarcastically—"you all know how headstrong he can be. And that's why I'll need your help in this situation. I want to know how often he's seeing this young lady, where they go, and what they do. Obviously I can't follow him around, as I'm working all the time. But you boys have plenty of time on your hands."

"You want us to spy on C. M.?" Jackson gulped. He looked at his friends. "We can't do that to him."

"We *have* to do that," the third boy, a chubby teen named Andrew, insisted. "For his own sake."

Carter Morgan, Sr. nodded. "We all know that this girl can only bring Carter down to her level. I suppose you have some idea where they've been."

"I think I do, sir," Ted volunteered. "She works at that skateboard shop in town. You know, the one that surfer owns."

Carter Morgan, Sr.'s eyes grew dark. "I know the place only too well. Do you think he's been there?"

Ted shrugged. "I don't know. But it's a good place to start. After that, we'll have to search around. Carter doesn't tell us much these days."

"Yeah, we don't see him like we used to," Jackson agreed.

"We really miss him, sir," Ted added.

Carter Morgan, Sr. nodded. He knew exactly what this kid meant. Ted missed the free meals and drinks his grandson treated his prep-school friends to. And he probably missed the status he gained by hanging around with a member of the Morgan family. He'd seen Ted's type before.

Ordinarily, leeches like him made the old man ill. But in this case, Ted's desire to be part of Carter's circle would come in handy.

"Of course you'll be well compensated for your help," the old man said, pulling a checkbook from his desk drawer. "All I ask in return is as much information as you can give me."

Angie got home from work around six fifteen. She walked into the house, put her bookbag and her skateboard in the hall closet, and headed toward the kitchen, where she was certain her parents had already begun eating.

But that wasn't the case. Instead, her father was sitting in his chair, waiting for her like a lion about to pounce on its prey. "Where've you been?" he demanded in a deep, ominous voice.

"Work," Angie said. "You know that."

"I don't believe you," her father said. "I stopped by that store on my way home from work, and the place was closed up tight."

"Cody and I were both out giving lessons," Angie explained. She looked at her father curiously. "You stopped by the store? Why? Is everything okay? Is Mom all right?"

"She's fine, except she's real disappointed in you."

"In me? What'd I do?"

"Suppose you tell me," Charlie Simms barked out.

"What are you talking about?"

"I got called into my supervisor's office today," he told her. "He wanted to talk to me about my daughter's behavior. He told me it wasn't good for my career to have you fraternizing with the big boss's grandson. He said people were talking about the two of you. People had seen you . . . together."

Angie gulped. "What people?" she demanded.

"He didn't say. It doesn't matter, anyway." Charlie studied his daughter's face. "You aren't going to try to deny it, are you?"

"No. I'm not ashamed of it. I have been seeing Carter Morgan."

"Well, it's over now."

"Excuse me?" Angie demanded. "What business is it of yours?"

Charlie slammed his hand down on the table with such force that the floor shook. "I'm your father, damn it. That makes it my business."

"Nice of you to realize you're my father *now*. Where've you been for the past eighteen years?" She paused for a moment. "Oh yeah, sitting in that chair with your eyes glued to the TV. *Some father.*"

"I'm not going to take any lip from you, young lady. I want you to break off this ridiculous affair right now. *Or else!* I'm not going to have you be the reason I lose my job. I've worked too hard and too long."

"I don't have to take this crap from you," Angie spat back. "Carter's more important to me than you or your stupid job. You can just forget about breaking us up."

Charlie stared into her eyes. "What is it with you? First you want to go off to Philadelphia and be some great artist. Now you think you're worthy of dating a Morgan? When are you going to realize you're no better than the rest of us? The sooner you accept your lot in life, the happier you'll be."

"Oh, like you're so happy?" Angie demanded.

Her father was seething now. "Okay, Miss High-and-Mighty. You think you're better than me? You want to run with the powerful people? Well, let me show you who has power. Either you stop seeing Carter Morgan, or I tear up these," he vowed as he reached onto the table and picked up the packet of financial aid forms.

"You wouldn't dare," Angie barked at him.

"Watch me," Charlie answered. With a single flick of his wrist he ripped the packet of papers in two. He reached up and threw them in the air like confetti. "Bye-bye, school."

Angie gasped.

"*Never* underestimate me," her father said in a low, gravelly voice.

Angie turned and tore out the door of the house. She kept on running, down her block, past the school, the skate ramp, and the post office. She didn't know where she was going. She just knew she had to get out of there.

She ran until she found herself outside Sk8 4Ever. The shop was closed, but the light in Cody's apartment above the shop was still on. It was like a sign. A light in a storm. Cody would understand if anyone could. He'd help her and Carter. She just knew it. She wiped the burning tears from her eyes and headed up the stairs.

"Cody, Cody, please open up," she shouted, banging on the door. "Cody, are you there?"

The door opened slowly. Cody stood there in a red kimono, and obviously nothing else. "Angie," he said, surprised. "Um . . . I . . . this really isn't a good time, kiddo."

"But Cody, you're not going to believe what happened. Please. I have to get out of here. I'm suffocating. You must understand. You know how much freedom means."

"Can't we talk about this tomorrow?" Cody seemed rather uncomfortable.

In a moment, it became clear why he'd tried to get rid of her. Dodo came to the door, buttoning her blouse and straightening her skirt. "Angie. What's wrong, *ma cherie*?"

Angie didn't even question her aunt's presence at Cody's place. Instead, she fell gratefully into her arms and let her story pour out with her tears. The words came quickly. She was anxious to release the pain of rejection she'd had to endure from Buzz, her friends, Carter's grandfather, and even her own father.

Dodo listened, gently rocking Angie back and forth, comforting her the way she'd wished her own mother would've comforted *her* so many years ago. When she was certain her niece had said all she needed to, she kissed the top of her head gently. "So what do you want to do?" she asked her.

"I don't know."

"Well, you have a few options."

"I have no options!" Angie exclaimed. "Haven't you been listening? Dad's trapped me here. He won."

"Not necessarily," Dodo said calmly. "You could solve all of this, make everyone happy. All you have to do is stop seeing Carter."

Angie stared at her aunt in disbelief. That wasn't what she'd expected from Dodo. "I won't do that. I can't do that. He . . . I . . . *no!* That's not an option. Sure, other people would be happy. But Carter and I would never survive without each other."

Dodo smiled proudly at her niece. "You would survive," she assured her. "But I'm glad you're not willing to roll over and play dead for a bunch of narrowminded jerks. Sorry to say that about your dad, Angie."

"Don't apologize for the truth."

"Well, anyway, I'm glad you've found Carter," Dodo said.

"I'm going to need him if I'm going to be stuck in Torren for the rest of my life."

"Who said you're going to be stuck here? You'll go to Philadelphia in the spring like you planned."

"But how? I don't have any money."

"You'll figure out a way," Cody interrupted. "Don't let them keep you down. You have a dream—follow it. I did."

"So did I," Dodo added.

"Yeah, but you wound up back here anyway," Angie reminded her aunt.

"I had some unfinished business," Dodo reminded her. "I *chose* to return. And you might too, someday." She laughed at Angie's expression. "Don't look so shocked. You don't know what the future holds for you. Only I know that," she teased.

"And my future has Philadelphia in it?" Angie asked hopefully.

"If you want it to," Dodo told her. "But you'll have to work hard for what you want. Just like I did. Just like Cody did. Only you'll have it easier than we did."

"How?"

"Because you have something we didn't," Cody suggested.

"What's that?"

Dodo wrapped her arm around Angie's shoulders. "Us."

16

The next few weeks were a flurry of stolen moments and secret hiding places. Carter and Angie met at the old skate ramp and visited diners in small towns in the mountains, where Carter was sure his grandfather didn't know a soul. Before they knew it, Christmas was less than a week away.

Angie wasn't looking forward to the holidays this year. She knew how lonely they would be. Her father barely spoke to her anymore, and while his silence hadn't bothered her in the past, it really cut her now. Her mother tried to talk to her, but Angie knew that they both sensed that the riff between them had grown too wide for either of them to ever cross, even at Christmas.

As for the kids at school, Angie knew where they'd be for the holiday—getting drunk at

Zack's parents' Christmas Eve tree-trimming party. For the past few years, Angie had been there too, drinking eggnog, hanging tinsel, and exchanging cheap gifts with her friends. But this year, she knew she'd be excluded from the celebration. She'd barely even seen Buzz or the others since that day at Sk8 4Ever. She'd heard talk that they'd been building a makeshift ramp on the empty lot Carter Morgan had bought for his auxiliary mill offices. Apparently, the kids were determined to put a skatepark there one way or another. Angie had been pretty proud of Buzz when she'd heard what he'd done. It took guts for him to spit in the old man's face that way. But of course she hadn't tried to tell him that. He'd never listen to her now, anyway.

So far, Angie hadn't heard that Carter Morgan, Sr. had done anything to stop the ramp. But Angie knew that wouldn't last long. He wasn't going to give in to a bunch of skaters. Carter Morgan always took what he wanted, when he wanted it.

Like he was taking Carter away from her—at least for the holidays. The Morgan family would be off skiing at their place in Aspen, Colorado, from just before Christmas Eve straight through New Year's. Which basically left Angie completely alone. Of course there was always Aunt Dodo and Cody, but Angie didn't want to intrude on them. They never treated her like she was unwelcome, of course, but nothing could make you feel more like a third wheel than being with two people who had shared experiences far different from your own. Being with Dodo and Cody meant enduring an evening of obscure references to the Beach Boys, the Grateful Dead, the Doors, and Chad and Jeremy lyrics.

Carter knew Angie was disappointed about his being away, so he'd surprised her with plans for them to celebrate their own Christmas—even if it was a week early. He'd arranged for them to have a complete goose dinner at a small inn near a ski resort. It was pretty far from Torren, but Carter had promised it was worth the drive. Angie didn't mind riding along the mountain roads with Carter—she'd actually grown fond of the intimate privacy the small car offered.

But before they headed for the inn, Angie had a surprise of her own. On Sunday morning she waited excitedly for him to pull into the parking lot outside Opal's. She could barely contain herself as the car came into view. She ran toward the driver's side of his car. "Move over," she ordered. "I'm taking the wheel today."

"Excuse me?" Carter asked. "Do you even have a license?"

"Well, a permit," Angie admitted. "I never actually took the road test. But *I'm* driving today."

Carter shook his head. "I don't think that's such a good idea, Angie."

"You don't trust me with your car?"

"It's not that. Well, actually, it *is* that," Carter admitted. "And besides, you don't know how to get to the restaurant."

"Oh, you can drive to the restaurant. We've got a stop to make before we go there. Now move over."

Carter sighed and did as he was told. He'd learned long ago not to argue with Angie when she set her chin in that determined way.

Angie gleefully slid into the driver's seat and gunned the little car.

"Whoa, slow down," Carter warned her as she sped down the highway.

"Spoilsport," she teased. "Where's your sense of adventure?"

"I think I left it on that last turn you made."

"Relax, we're almost there." She made another hairpin turn and pulled into a gravelly driveway. "This is it," she announced, turning off the engine and getting out of the car.

Carter looked at the small cottage at the edge of the driveway. A large neon sign in the window read THE HOLE IMAGE. "This is *what*?" he asked her.

"Your Christmas present, silly."

"You got me a hole?"

Angie nodded. "In your ear. Your left earlobe to be exact. Now hurry up and get out of the car. We have a nine-thirty appointment with Jerry. He's the best. I was lucky to get him. We can't be late."

"An earring?" Carter asked her dubiously. "You got me a piercing for Christmas?"

"Come on. Nothing's sexier than a guy with a pierced ear."

"If you say so."

"I say so."

"Does it hurt?" he asked nervously.

"Nah. Just a pinch. Trust me. It hurts a lot less in your ear than it does in your eyebrow. Or at least that's what people tell me. You should've heard LeeAnn screaming when she got that done."

Carter winced. "Is it clean? I mean, can't you get diseases and stuff?"

"It's clean. He pierces you with prepackaged single-use needles and then puts in an earring made of surgical titanium that comes in a sealed bag. You won't get any diseases. I've done this tons of times."

"Twelve," Carter told her. "Six in each ear. I've counted. But . . ."

"Come on, you big baby. You're not going to reject my Christmas gift, are you, Scrooge?"

Carter knew when he was beat. Reluctantly, he got out of the car and followed Angie toward the cottage.

If Carter was nervous before they stepped inside, he really began to panic when he met Jerry. He was a big man, nearly six foot six, with a potbelly and big arms that were canvasses for at least five tattoos each. In his ear were several piercings, including one that was a huge plastic cylinder.

"This the victim?" Jerry teased. He seemed slightly taken aback by the kind of kid Carter was. He didn't get a whole lot of rich preppies stopping by. And he certainly didn't expect to see one of them walking in with Angie Simms.

"His name's Carter. It's his first time, Jer, so be gentle," Angie joked.

"Okay," Jerry agreed. "Unless he's *into* pain. Are you, Carter?"

He shook his head nervously.

"Okay, come on in the back room. Hurry up. I've got another appointment right after you."

Angie sat down on the red velvet sofa in the waiting room. "Aren't you coming?" Carter asked Angie anxiously.

"No, she stays out here," Jerry told him. "It's just you and me behind the curtain, big guy."

When Carter emerged a few minutes later, his face was a little bit pale, but he was grinning. "That wasn't so bad," he said, turning so Angie could see the small blue titanium hoop in his left ear. "So, am I sexy or what?"

"I can hardly hold myself back," she said, leaping at him and kissing him wildly.

"Hey, take it somewhere else, willya?" Jerry teased. "I got customers here. You sure I can't give you another piercing, Angie? Maybe a belly ring or something?"

"Not today. Thanks anyway, Jer. Merry Christmas!"

Angie could tell Carter was pleased with her gift. During the drive to the restaurant she caught him checking out his ear from time to time in the rearview mirror.

"You like it, huh?" she asked him finally.

"It's kind of cool," he admitted.

"It's gonna really piss your grandfather off," Angie warned.

"So what else is new? Everything I do pisses him off."

"You think he knows we're still together?"

"I don't know," Carter mused. "Maybe. But he's been keeping his mouth shut."

"Maybe he's figured out he can't do anything to stop it," Angie suggested hopefully.

"I'm not so sure," he warned. "It's not like him to surrender. But don't worry. He can't beat us. It's two against one. The sooner he faces that, the better." He placed a strong hand on Angie's leg, and she felt a tingle race straight through her body, a wild electrical current of excitement. She leaned over and cuddled against his chest as he drove.

The traditional dinner was everything Carter had promised and more. Angie had never had Christmas goose with all the trimmings before. She thought it was just something people in those Dickens books did. Up until this dinner, Angie had assumed that everyone had ham on Christmas, the way her friends and family always did. But apparently people like Carter had goose, with mashed potatoes and string bean almondine.

"That was unbelievable," she told him, sighing contentedly as she nibbled the last bit of crispy skin.

"How about dessert?" Carter asked. "They make the most incredible bread pudding here. Lots of cinnamon on top."

"I don't think I can eat another thing." She twisted his wrist slightly to get a glimpse at the face of his watch. "Besides, it's getting late. We should probably be leaving."

Carter pulled his hand away from hers and clumsily reached into his pants pocket. "In a minute," he said nervously. "I just want to give you something." He brought his hand up to the table and placed a small box in front of her. "Merry Christmas."

Angie stared at the box. It was so beautiful— navy blue with gold trim and a tiny gold bow on top.

"Aren't you going to open it?" he asked her, sounding more nervous with each passing second.

Gingerly, she lifted the lid of the box. "Oh my God," she whispered as she gently removed a thin gold ring and held it up. Three small blue sapphires sparkled up at her. It looked as though they were dancing in the candlelight. "Carter, it's beautiful."

"It's a promise ring," he explained. "A vow that I'll always be there for you. The stones stand for yesterday, today, and tomorrow."

"I don't know what to say."

"Say you'll wear it."

She slid the ring onto her finger and smiled with surprise. "It's a perfect fit."

"Your aunt Dodo helped me," Carter admitted. "She traced the inside of one of your rings, and I took her tracing to a jeweler." He seemed pleased that his plan had worked out so well.

"I love it," she told him. "I'm never going to take it off." She reached across the table and kissed him.

Just then the waiter stopped by the table. "Can I get you anything else?" he asked them.

"I've got everything I need," Angie told him, her eyes never leaving Carter's.

"Okay then, here's your check," the waiter said. "Say, do you kids have far to go to get home?"

"About two hours. We're heading back to Torren," Carter replied. "Why?"

"There's no way you'll get there now," the waiter said. "It's snowing really hard. Didn't you hear there was a blizzard heading this way?"

Angie's heart began to pound. They hadn't been listening to the radio in the car, so they hadn't heard any weather reports. "A *blizzard*?" she repeated.

"Yeah, it's coming from the east. They're closing all the roads. You guys better find someplace to go that's close."

The waiter walked off, leaving Angie and Carter dumbfounded. "What are we going to do?" she asked him nervously.

"Well, we're not far from my dad's cabin," Carter said slowly. "We could spend the night together there." He stopped himself. "I didn't mean that the way it sounded."

"I know what you meant," she assured him. "I think it's a lucky thing the cabin's nearby. But we'd better get going. You heard what the waiter said about the roads."

Surprisingly, the Morgan's cabin wasn't anything fancy. It was little more than an overgrown version of the log cabins Angie had built with her Lincoln Logs when she was a kid. There was a single living room with a big fireplace in the middle. Off to the side was a kitchenette. There were three doors leading off from the living room. Angie figured those were the bedrooms and the bathroom.

"It's nothing like I expected," Angie murmured, looking around.

"I know it's not really anything special," Carter apologized. "My dad had it built years ago. He used to use it to get away from my grandfather, I think. Once in a while he and I would come up here to go fishing. But he doesn't visit here much anymore. And I haven't been here in years. I'm surprised I remembered how to get to the place, actually."

Angie grinned, imagining Carter as a little boy fishing with his dad. The endearing image made her feel even closer to him. She wished she could have seen him then, all proud and excited at having a really big one caught on the line. He must've been adorable.

"I love it here," she told him honestly. "It's not all showy and fancy. It's just a log cabin in the woods. It fits you."

Carter sighed with relief. He'd so wanted her to love this place as much as he did. "I've never brought anyone up here before. My friends wouldn't like it very much. They expect . . . well, you know. This place is heated by a fireplace and a stove. And the rooms are kind of small and bare. There isn't even a phone."

"Hey," Angie said. "We should probably call home and let our parents know where we are. Not that mine really care . . ."

Carter pulled out his camera phone. "You're right. Only . . . no service."

Angie checked her phone. "Mine, too. This place *is* rustic," she said, shivering.

"You're all wet," Carter noted. "Let me get you a blanket."

"I think there might still be a robe in the closet." He headed out of the living room and walked through one of the doors. A moment later, he came out with a wool blanket and a child-size, well-worn, plaid flannel robe.

"The robe was mine when I was about thirteen. It'll probably fit you, though." He pointed to the middle door. "The bathroom's right through there." He glanced over to a well-stocked pile of wood by the fireplace. It had a few cobwebs on it, but the wood seemed dry. "I'll light a fire while you change."

"You're all wet too. What're you going to do?"

"I'll be okay. I'll dry off by the fire pretty quickly. Now go on. I don't want you getting sick."

"But—"

"Go change," Carter ordered. "Let me take care of you, will you?"

Let me take care of you. Angie had spent so much time taking care of herself that the thought of someone else helping with the burden was overwhelming. She wrapped her arms around him and hugged him gratefully.

"What's this for?" he asked her.

"I don't know. Just because?"

"Works for me," he laughed, returning the warmth of her embrace until he noticed the goosebumps up and down her arms. "Will you go dry off? I've got 'man's' work over here." He lowered his voice to a deep boom, and pretended to flex his muscles like a bodybuilder.

Angie giggled and did as he said. She walked into the bathroom and changed out of her wet clothes. She slipped the robe on, trying to imagine the tall, muscular Carter being young enough to fit in the small stretch of plaid flannel. It was hard to picture.

Looking at the mirror in the dim bathroom light, she could see that her face was a maze of eyeliner and mascara. *So much for waterproof,* she thought ruefully as she began to scrub her face clean.

Suddenly the lights went out. *"Carter!"* Angie screamed, running out of the bathroom. "The lights!"

"It's okay," he replied calmly as he placed another log on the fire. "The power just went out. Probably because of the storm. It's no big deal; we have plenty of candles."

Angie flopped down on the couch, embarrassed by her sudden show of cowardice. She watched as Carter went into the kitchenette and pulled out a box of candles. He went around the room, lighting them one by one.

If the cabin had been rustic and beautiful before, it was a magical place under candlelight. The bright orange flames cast a golden glow on the wooden walls. Shadows on the wall danced with the movement of the flames, like a perfect ballet playing out against the soundtrack of the burning logs in the fire.

Once all the candles were lit, Carter took off his wet shirt and hung it over a chair to dry. She watched him intently, fascinated by the fluidness of his movements. Eventually, he felt her eyes on him and looked over toward the couch. As he caught a glimpse of Angie sitting there in the candlelight, his expression changed slightly. "Wow."

"What?"

"You just look so different."

"I do? What do you mean?"

"It's just that I've never seen you without your makeup before. You look so . . . so . . . innocent."

Angie blushed. She was more innocent than he could imagine. She was actually kind of amazed by her reaction to her current situation. Here she was, alone in the woods with a boy, and she wasn't at all nervous or afraid. Being in this cabin, just her and Carter, seemed the most natural thing in the world. There was no other place she'd ever want to be. Slowly she got up from the couch and walked over toward him, her eyes gazing longingly into his as she sat beside him in front of the fire.

Carter studied her expression oddly, unsure of what to do next. Angie knew he would never ask any more of her than she was willing to give. Maybe that was why she suddenly *felt* so willing. In the flash of an instant it all became clear. Her whole life had led her to this moment, alone in this place with this person.

This was where she was meant to be. *To always be.* She reached out her arms and pulled him toward her.

The current surged through both their bodies, and the power of it was beyond their control. Angie was overwhelmed by the passion of it all, as her body experienced sensations she could never even have imagined. It was as though she was in a fog—a magnificent haze from which she never wanted to escape.

Carter stopped kissing her long enough to make certain that this was what she really wanted. He never wanted her to regret anything she shared with him. "Angie?" he asked gently. "Are you sure?"

She nodded slowly. She'd never been surer of anything in her entire life. "Yesterday, today, and tomorrow," she murmured, as she slowly untied her robe.

Angie squinted against the light as she opened her eyes. The morning sun shone bright through the windows of the cabin. She shivered slightly from the cold and wrapped the thick wool blanket tighter around her. She rolled over, expecting to find Carter sleeping beside her, but he was nowhere to be found.

"Carter," she called out cheerfully, sitting up in front of the dwindling fire.

There was no answer.

"Carter?" Angie jumped to her feet and held the blanket tighter as she walked around the cabin. But Carter wasn't there. She peeked out the window. The snow was piled high against the cabin, but a clear path had been dug to the main road. Tire tracks could be seen along the path.

Carter was gone.

A sudden panic came over Angie. Could he have left her here alone? No, Carter wouldn't do that, she assured herself. Not after everything they had said . . . and done.

Then where was he?

A million horrifying thoughts raced through her mind. Who knew what kind of crazies lived out here in the woods? There were all those ghost stories about crazies named Cropsy or the Jersey Devil or something. They all lived in the woods far from civilization. Sure, they were all just make-believe, but those stories had to come from somewhere. What if some insane-asylum escapee had gotten to Carter? Worse yet, what if one of his grandfather's sick minions had kidnapped him as punishment for his relationship with her? What if . . . Angie raced into the bathroom, where she'd left her clothes the night before. They were still damp, but not too bad. She threw them on hastily and went back into the living room to find her backpack. She pulled out her phone, but then remembered she couldn't reach him.

Now she was snowbound in a cabin in God knows where, with no phone, no food, no heat, *no Carter.*

Just then a blast of cold air burst into the cabin. "Good morning, sleepyhead," Carter greeted her as he made his way over a mound of snow.

Angie didn't know whether to hug him or kill him. She decided to go with the former. "Thank God!" she exclaimed, leaping into his arms.

"Whoa, hold on, this stuff's hot," he said, reaching over to place two steaming cups of coffee on the counter.

Angie looked over at the drinks. "Coffee?" she shouted. "You left me here for *coffee?*"

"I figured you'd want something to warm you up before the drive back. The roads are all cleared now."

"I thought you were dead or something." She regretted the words as soon as they left her mouth. She sounded like some sort of raving lunatic. But she couldn't help herself. She hugged him harder. "What if I'd lost you?"

He bent down and kissed the top of her head. "That's not happening, Angie."

They stood quietly for a moment, wrapped in a blissful embrace. "We should really start getting back," he said finally.

"Do we have to?"

Carter sighed. "I think so. It's getting late." He turned his wrist to look at his gold watch, but his arm was bare. "Damn!"

"What?"

"I lost my watch."

"Are you sure? Maybe it's around here somewhere." She started to search under the chairs and couch.

"It was sitting here," he said, pointing to a table near the fire. "I could've sworn I put it on this morning. That latch probably broke some-where. I'll bet it's buried under a mound of snow by now. Man, my father's going to kill me. That Rolex cost him a fortune."

Angie wondered what a fortune would be to someone like Carter Morgan II. She assumed it was a whole hell of a lot. She began to search the other rooms of the cabin, folding blankets and placing them on the beds as she searched.

"What are you doing?"

"Cleaning up," she replied simply.

That shocked him. "You're amazing, you know that?"

"Let me guess, the girls you know don't think to clean up when they've been a guest in someone's home."

"Probably not."

"You know, for rich people, your friends don't have a whole lot of class."

Carter couldn't argue with that. Instead he grabbed the other end of the blanket and helped her fold. "This is nice," he said as he grabbed the ends and placed the folded blanket on the couch. "Kind of like playing house."

Angie felt a warmness rush through her. She'd felt the same thing, but had been afraid to say it. She hadn't wanted to sound all mushy or anything like that. She was awfully glad he'd said it instead.

But they both knew that they would have to leave and head back into reality. It was bound to be a pretty *ugly* reality at that. They'd been gone all night, and no one knew where they were. Even Angie's absent parents would notice that. And who knew what kind of reaction a control freak like Carter Morgan, Sr. would have to Carter's disappearance? There were going to be plenty of questions for them to answer back in Torren.

17

Carter dropped Angie off in front of her house. She'd tried to convince him to just leave her at Opal's, but he'd insisted on seeing her home safely. He didn't want her trying to make her way through the heavy snowdrifts without boots.

She watched as he drove off, procrastinating for as long as she could before heading into her house. Finally, she started to make her way up the driveway. *Time to face the inquisition.*

The front door was slightly ajar. Angie pushed it open and walked in, hoping against hope that her parents were still asleep. It was a Monday, but Angie had seen her dad's car in the driveway. They'd probably closed the mill because of the blizzard. Maybe her folks had taken advantage of the fact that they could get a little extra shut-eye.

But that wasn't the case at all. Everyone in the house was wide awake. As Angie walked into the living room, her mother leaped off the couch. "Angie!" she exclaimed, rushing over to hug her daughter. "You're all right."

"See, I told you," Dodo said, walking into the living room. "She was just waiting out the storm at a friend's house. Right, Angie?"

Angie nodded gratefully in her aunt's direction, fully aware that Dodo knew just who that friend was. "I tried to call, but my phone wouldn't work."

"Your mother never believes me," Dodo said. "You'd think by now she'd have learned."

"I thought you'd been in that fire. I was sure . . ." Her mother's voice drifted off.

"Fire? What fire?" Angie asked.

"On that abandoned lot by the mill," her mother explained.

"Your deadbeat friends nearly burnt down the whole mill," Angie's father added, coming down the stairs in just his pajama bottoms, his oversize belly bulging over the top. "It's closed till they can get things up and running again. I'm losing at least a week's pay thanks to those delinquents. And right before Christmas, too."

"My friends? What friends? *What happened?*"

Dodo put her arm around Angie. "There was a fire at that makeshift skatepark Buzz and some of the others built next to the mill," she explained as gently as she could. "The ramp collapsed."

"I heard one of them was hurt real bad," Angie's mother said. "When you didn't come home, I thought maybe you were under . . . maybe they hadn't found you yet."

"I'm fine, Mom, honest," Angie assured her. She turned to her aunt. "Who's in the hospital?"

"Cody said it was Buzz," Dodo said calmly. "He's on his way over there now."

Buzz! "I've got to go see him," Angie exclaimed.

"I thought you two were on the outs," her mother recalled.

"I've known him forever—I've got to go see him," Angie insisted again, her jaw set firmly.

"I'll get my keys and drive you there," Dodo volunteered. "You'll never get there walking through all this snow. Come on."

Angie followed her out of the house and to the garage. Dodo got in the driver's side and pulled up the button on the passenger door. Angie climbed in and buckled up.

They drove along in silence for a while, as

Dodo let her niece digest all the information that had just been thrown at her. But there was something she had to make sure of. "So you and Carter found someplace to go?" she asked, implying that she knew full well what had happened last night.

"Yeah. His dad's got a cabin in the mountains. We didn't plan it. We were just going out to dinner, and then the blizzard started. We got there just before they closed the roads."

Dodo nodded quietly. "So how do you feel?"

"Different, I guess." Angie answered her aunt's question without shame or guilt. "Warmer . . . older . . . complete. It's kind of hard to put into words."

Dodo smiled. "You described it perfectly. But Angie . . ." She stammered for a moment, trying to find a way to broach the subject.

Angie studied her aunt curiously. Dodo was always so sure of herself. It was strange to see her so uncomfortable. "What is it?"

Dodo took a deep breath. "Look, I'm not asking any questions, okay? The details of something like this are best kept to yourself. I respect that. I do. But, just promise me that you were smart about this."

So that's what's worrying her. "Carter would

never have it any other way. He would never let *anything* happen to me, Aunt Dodo. And you know I'm too smart not to be safe."

"Good thing he was thinking ahead," Dodo said with just a touch of cynicism. From her change in tone, it was clear she was concerned that Carter might have been more devious about setting up the situation than Angie suspected.

But Angie knew that couldn't be further from the truth. "Actually, it wasn't Carter who had protection, it was me," Angie told her.

"You?"

"On Halloween, LeeAnn was giving out condoms to everyone like they were candy. We thought it was hysterical. I threw mine in my purse and almost forgot about it until . . ."

"Good old LeeAnn," Dodo chuckled, relieved.

LeeAnn. Angie's mind switched gears suddenly, clicking back to the fire at the ramp. "Is she okay?"

Dodo nodded. "She was a real hero. She pulled Zack away from the ramp just before it fell on him. But Buzz wasn't so lucky. He took the brunt of it."

Tears stung in Angie's eyes. "He isn't going to die, is he?" she asked anxiously.

"He'll pull through," Dodo promised her. She was silent for a minute, trying to come up with a way to reveal the upsetting news to her niece. "But Angie," she said slowly, "he's going to have a hard time of it. It'll be a while before he can walk again. And even then he's not going to be the same. His mother told Cody that he'll never be able to skateboard again."

Buzz was lying quietly in his hospital bed with an intravenous tube attached to his left arm when Angie entered the room. His left leg was raised slightly in some sort of traction device. Other than the dark bruise on one of his cheeks, he looked like the same old Buzz— although the mischievous glint in his eyes had been replaced by a dull stare. Angie hoped it was just the medication.

"Buzz," she said quietly, sitting in the chair beside the bed. "I'm so sorry."

He turned his head slowly in her direction. "Angie, what're you doing here?"

"I came as soon as I heard."

"You just heard now?" He glanced up at the clock on the wall. It was almost noon. "Where were you all night?" He paused a moment. "Never mind. It doesn't matter anymore."

"Does it hurt?" she asked, not knowing what else to say.

"They've got me pretty doped up," he said. "But not doped up enough."

"What do you mean?"

"I'm clear enough to know that my life's over."

"No it's not. You'll be up and around in no time. The doctor said so." She tried to sound as cheerful as she could. But Buzz wasn't fooled by her bravado.

"I wish I'd died in that damn fire," he told her.

"Don't say that, Buzz. You don't mean it."

"It's all been taken away from me, Angie. You know that. You get that better than anyone."

Angie *did* understand. Skateboarding was what made Buzz special. He may not have been a great student, or captain of the football team, or the lead singer in a band. But on the board, he was king. He stood out from the pack. His style at the ramp was how he earned his respect. Now he was just another millbrat with nothing to look forward to but a life like the rest of them.

"Buzz, it'll be okay," she soothed him. "There's a whole world out there. You'll find something else. You know what Cody always says. There are lots of paths to freedom."

Buzz shook his head. "Not for me."

"Buzz."

"Look, Angie, get out of here, okay? I don't need your pity."

"I'm not—"

"You weren't there when it happened. There's no reason for you to be here now. You've moved on. I get it."

Angie shook her head. She hadn't moved on by herself. He'd pushed her away. But now wasn't the time to remind him of that. What would be the point? "Buzz, I'm your friend. I want to be here for you."

"I said get out!" He turned away.

Angie could see his body shake a little as he tried to smother the sound of his sobs. Angie knew the last thing he would have wanted was for her to see him cry. If Buzz wouldn't take her offer of friendship, she could at least leave him his dignity. She owed him that much.

Quietly, Angie turned and left the room.

Carter Morgan, Sr. sat behind his huge desk and picked up the phone. Quickly, he dialed the now-familiar number and waited for an answer.

"Hello?"

"Nice job, Ted," the old man said into the receiver. "There was only minimal damage to the mill. And the insurance will easily cover that. I'm very impressed with your work."

"So when do I get the money?"

"I'll meet you here tomorrow morning, before the school day begins," the old man promised. "You'll get the first half then."

"Just *half*? But I did exactly what you told me to do."

"And it worked out better than I could have expected. But you haven't completed the mission, have you? My grandson is still seeing that trash. When that's over, you'll get the rest of your money."

"How'm I supposed to get her away from him if even you couldn't do it?"

"I'm sure you'll think of something," Carter Morgan, Sr. replied. "You're a very bright boy."

18

It was hard for Angie to get to sleep on the first Saturday night after New Year's. Tomorrow was Sunday, and she and Carter would be escaping for the day. She hadn't seen him in nearly three weeks. It seemed like an eternity.

When sleep finally did come, Angie was restless. Her dreams were horrid. She and Carter were on opposite sides of a river that kept growing wider and wider until she couldn't see him anymore. Then it was Carter being pulled away from her by wolves as she stood by, helpless and unable to free him.

The dreams were so bad that she was grateful when her cell phone rang at six thirty in the morning. She was relieved to hear Carter's voice on the other end. He made her feel safe again.

"Angie, hi. I'm sorry to wake you up so early."

"Mmm," she moaned, blinking twice to get the sleep out of her eyes. "I missed you."

"I missed you, too."

"Thank God it's Sunday," she replied sleepily. "What time do you want to meet?"

"That's the thing, Angie. We can't get together today."

She was awake now. "Why not?"

"It's not my fault," Carter assured her. "I was looking forward to today. But my grandfather is insisting that I go to this town meeting."

"A town meeting? On a Sunday? They never have meetings on Sundays."

"It's an emergency meeting."

"Why would your grandfather want you there?"

"A show of family support," Carter sighed. "But you might want to be there too. The meeting's about skateboarding. My grandfather and some of his cronies on the town council want it outlawed."

"What?!" Angie shouted out, forgetting what time it was. The last thing she wanted was to wake her parents now.

"He's all hyped up about that fire," Carter

explained. "It happened on his property."

"That's no reason to try to get rid of skate-boarding altogether."

"Well, Angie, you have to agree that was a pretty stupid stunt Buzz and Zack pulled. I mean, setting a fire . . ."

"They didn't set that fire," Angie told him firmly.

"Come on, Angie, they were the only ones around."

"How stupid do you think they are?" Angie argued. "Why would they set a fire and then wait for it to burn around them?"

"I don't know," Carter answered. "Maybe it went out of control too fast, or maybe—"

"You know, maybe if your grandfather had let Cody buy that land and build a safe skatepark, none of this would have happened. It's really his fault, you know."

"My grandfather's fault? Are you kidding?" Cody demanded. "It was his property that got torched."

"You're defending him now?"

Carter took a deep breath. "I don't want to fight with you, Angie," he said slowly. "There are enough people angry with me right now."

She was silent for a moment. He was right.

Other than Cody and Dodo, there was no one else in their corner. Each of them was really all the other had. "Okay. What time's the meeting?"

"Two thirty. Right in the middle of the day. That's why we can't get together. He's going to be watching me to make sure I'm around when the family leaves for the meeting."

"I guess I'll be at the meeting too, then. Someone's going to have to stand up for our rights." Somehow she didn't think Zack, George, LeeAnn, and Gina would be able to plead the case too effectively. Buzz might have, but he was still in the hospital, learning to use his weakened legs.

"It's going to be so hard, seeing you there and not being able to be near you," Carter told her sincerely.

She knew what he meant. Having him be so close and yet so far away would surely cause her a physical ache.

The town hall was full of people when Angie arrived that afternoon. Most of them were clearly on Carter Morgan, Sr.'s side. And not just the rich folks, either. A lot of the mill-workers were showing their support for the owner of their place of employment. What a joke that was. In their own circles—at the small, smoky bars and fast-food joints they frequented—they would sit for hours trashing the mill's owner and everything he stood for. But today they were all here to offer him their support in the hopes that it would somehow help their careers. Angie wasn't at all surprised to see her own father sitting there among the hypocrites. Luckily, he didn't seem to see her.

But Carter did. Their eyes met the minute she entered the hall. He was sitting right beside his grandfather, dressed in an expensive wool sportscoat and gray slacks. His outfit was almost identical to that of the tall, graying man on the other side of him. Angie was pretty sure that was his father. He looked quite a bit like Carter, except his eyes looked tired and lifeless, and he slumped slightly in his seat.

A slight shiver went through Angie as she realized that Carter could wind up like that in a few years if they didn't get out of Torren soon. She turned away, anxious to shake the image of Carter's defeated father from her mind.

The skaters sat on the other side of the aisle. Not surprisingly, there were quite a few of them. Zack, George, LeeAnn, and Gina were there, of course, but there were also a number of skaters from surrounding towns who had come to Torren to show their support for their sport and way of life.

Cody and Dodo were sitting near the back, just a few rows behind the crowd of skaters. Dodo was wearing a plain black suede skirt and one of her long flowing blouses. Cody was actually wearing a sport jacket and a tie. His long hair was pulled back neatly, and his beard had been trimmed. It was the first time Angie had ever seen her boss dressed up.

"Wow! Look at you," she said as she slid into the row beside her aunt and Cody.

"He cleans up pretty nicely, doesn't he?" Dodo teased, fixing his tie slightly. Her eyes followed Cody's gaze. He was staring straight at Carter Morgan, Sr. "Forget it," she told him quietly. "He's not going to look over here. He's pretending we don't exist."

"What else is new?" Cody sighed. "He pretends, but he can't really ignore us. That's what's killing him."

"This meeting will now come to order!" Marcus Beinder, the town's mayor, declared, banging his gavel. He looked out at the crowd. "We've called this meeting to discuss the fire at

Morgan Mills, and what we can do to prevent something like that from happening again. There's a bill on the floor banning skateboarding, since it was a makeshift skateboard ramp on the property that went up in flames."

Carter Morgan, Sr. stood. "Mr. Mayor, I request an opportunity to speak."

The skaters leaped to their feet immediately and began to boo, trying to drown him out.

"Oh man," Cody groaned, burying his head in his hands. "They're playing right into his hands. He wants them to look like a bunch of wild animals. And they do."

"Order! Order!" Mayor Beinder demanded, pounding his gavel. "One more outburst like that and I'll have you all thrown out." He turned to the owner of Morgan Mills. "The chair recognizes Carter Morgan, Sr."

"Thank you, Mr. Mayor. As you know, there was a four-alarm fire on my property just before the Christmas holiday. It caused a tremendous amount of damage. Not only was the empty lot burned, but the mill beside it was damaged as well. I had to close down my business for three days."

"All right!" A crowd of skateboarders cheered the idea of Mr. Morgan losing business.

"Order! Order!" the mayor demanded.

"It wasn't just me who lost money during that period," Carter Morgan, Sr. continued. He waved his hand in the direction of the workers who had come to sit behind him and kiss up to his cash. "These folks lost their wages as well. Right before the holidays. And whose fault was that? The people who started the fire in the first place." He turned and glared in the direction of the skaters.

"We don't know for sure who started that fire," Mayor Beinder reminded him.

"We have an idea," Carter Morgan, Sr. replied. "The same hooligans who have been bringing this town down for years. Skateboarders bring nothing but trouble to Torren. They always have. For a while, it was only petty crimes. Now it's hundreds of thousands of dollars worth of damage. I demand that we outlaw this sport—and I use the term 'sport' loosely—before I, and the people of Torren, lose another cent."

That last bit was too much for Angie to take. She leaped out of her chair and raced to the front of the room, ready to confront Carter Morgan, Sr. face to face. "You heartless creep!" she shouted in his face. "Money. That's all you think about. There's a boy lying in a hospital bed right now because of the fire on your property, and you haven't even called once to check on him."

"Now why would I do that? He was trespassing on my land. Can I help it if he became the victim of his own mischief?" Mr. Morgan demanded.

"You blame all this on skateboarders, but you have no proof that any of them started that fire!" Angie insisted. "In fact, I read in the newspaper that not one of them was found with so much as a match on them when they were brought into the hospital."

Carter Morgan, Sr. looked in the direction of his friend, Sheriff Martin. The sheriff frowned and then shrugged. Angie was definitely correct about those facts.

"Oh come on," Carter Morgan, Sr. replied with an air of superiority that angered Angie even more. "If they didn't start it, who did?"

"There are plenty of people who hate you enough to start a fire at that mill. People who might kiss your ass to your face, but spit at you when you walk away. Despite what you may think, you're not very loved around here, Mr. Morgan." She turned slightly and caught a glimpse of *her* Carter. He was staring at her with

271

a face that broadcast both surprise and pride. She could tell he was impressed with the way she was standing up to his grandfather. He'd never been able to do that. Nobody had.

Carter's show of unspoken support gave her the courage to say the things she'd been holding in for as long as she could remember. "Skateboarding isn't the problem in this town, Mr. Morgan. Your rich so-called friends are. They walk around acting like they're being charitable just by sharing Torren with people like us. But I have news for you, Mr. Morgan. You should be grateful that we're here. You've made your millions on our backs. If we turned on you, you'd be nothing, and you know it. That's why you want to take away skate-boarding. It's the one thing in this town you can't control. And somehow the idea of the people of Torren being out of your control scares the hell out of you!"

The skaters leaped to their feet again, applauding wildly, egging Angie on.

Mayor Beinder banged his gavel, hard. "Young lady, you are out of order! Now sit down!" he shouted over the screams and cheers of the skaters.

Finally things did settle down. As quiet took

over the hall, a small, dark-haired, roundish man in a suit stood up in the back of the room. He'd been sitting on Carter Morgan, Sr.'s side of the aisle, listening closely to what was being said. "May I address the meeting?" he asked the mayor.

Mayor Beinder eyed the stranger cautiously. "And your name is, sir?"

"I'm Michael Schwartz," the man replied. "I represent the American Civil Liberties Union. I received word of this meeting, and came down from Harrisburg. I just want to let you know that should your town try to pass an ordinance banning all forms of skateboarding, the ACLU is prepared to fight it—all the way to the Supreme Court if necessary."

A collective gasp sounded in the room. Angie looked around. Everyone seemed surprised at the statement. Everyone other than her aunt Dodo, that is. She sat tall in her chair, apparently extremely pleased with herself.

Carter Morgan, Sr. leaned back and whispered something to his team of lawyers. The lawyers shrugged.

"You'll never win that fight," the old man insisted.

Michael Schwartz shrugged. "Be that as it

may, we are prepared to fight vigorously in this matter. And I might add that while *we* have supporters all over the country who would gladly fund a battle for a fundamental freedom, the town of Torren would have to pay for its own defense using taxpayer dollars."

The mayor looked hopelessly at Carter Morgan, Sr. This was a no-win situation for him. He couldn't afford to offend the town's wealthiest and most powerful citizen, but the town could never afford to fight such a battle. And Carter Morgan, Sr., even with all his millions, couldn't match the funding of a national political organization.

"Perhaps we can compromise," the mayor suggested, obviously thinking as fast as he could. "Maybe we can ban skateboarding in certain areas, while still allowing it in other places."

Michael Schwartz nodded slowly. "Depending on the extent of the limits, I think that might work. We'll be in touch to see how your compromise works out." He picked up his briefcase and his overcoat and walked out of the building.

There was complete silence in the room as everyone watched him leave. For the first time, Carter Morgan, Sr. had been beaten. No one knew how to react.

But Mr. Morgan did. He stood again and said simply, "I thank you for your time, Mr. Mayor. And I look forward to seeing your ideas for your *compromise*." Then he turned and left the hall, his family straggling behind him. The skaters taunted the family as they walked by.

It killed Angie to see Carter walking out like that, part of the herd of sheep Old Man Morgan pushed around. She knew he didn't want to be there. He didn't agree with the feudal beliefs his grandfather had tried to indoctrinate the family with. He wasn't like the rest of them. She only wished everyone else could see the side of him that she did.

A few minutes later Angie found herself outside, surrounded by a group of skaters, all congratulating her on her performance. Unfortunately none of them were her former friends. Zack, George, LeeAnn, and Gina all stood by themselves, off to the side, whispering and watching as Angie spoke to the others of their kind.

Finally, Cody and Dodo walked over and helped Angie extricate herself from the crowd of well-wishers. "That was quite a performance," Cody congratulated her as they walked away. "It took a lot of guts."

"Not really," Angie said. "Someone had to stand up for Buzz. And he and I . . . well . . . we have a lot of history." She turned to her aunt Dodo. "So how'd you meet Michael Schwartz?"

Dodo laughed. "How did you know it was me who called him?"

"Just a hunch."

"Well, believe it or not, the esteemed Mr. Schwartz, Esquire, attends most of the psychic gatherings I go to. He's quite a hit with the paranormal crowd."

Angie was surprised. She never thought lawyers were into that sort of thing. *Another stereotype broken.* "So you told him about what was happening here?"

"I didn't have to," Dodo teased. "He just knew."

"Very funny." Angie laughed.

"Do you want to go home now?" Cody asked Angie. "I can give you a lift."

Home. That wasn't going to be pretty. Her father was going to kill her.

Dodo caught the look on her face. "You know what? You can stay with me tonight. That'll give Charlie a chance to cool down before you face him."

"Thanks," Angie said gratefully. She began

to follow her aunt and Cody toward the parking lot. But her path was soon blocked by Sheriff Martin.

"Angie Simms?" he asked her.

"Yes," she answered.

"I'd like to speak to you."

"What about?"

Sheriff Martin gave her an annoyed sigh, as though he couldn't believe any teenager—let alone a skater—would have the audacity to question him about anything. "You seem to be pretty certain that your friends over there didn't start this fire."

"I'm *completely* certain," Angie corrected him.

"I don't know how you can be so sure," the sheriff continued. "Unless you know something I don't. In which case, I'd like to talk to you."

"Sure," Angie agreed. "Would tomorrow be okay?"

"Tonight would be better."

Angie looked nervously over at Cody and Dodo. This didn't sound too good.

"It's okay, I'll come with you," Cody said calmly.

Dodo pulled out her cell phone. "I'll be

right behind you," she promised Angie. Then she spoke into the receiver. "Hello, Michael. I think I'm going to need a little more of your legal assistance. Can you meet my niece and me at the police station here in Torren?"

It had been a long night. By the time Angie arrived back at her aunt's apartment, it was nearly three o'clock in the morning. Still, she had to call Carter. This couldn't wait until morning. They had a big problem.

"Hello?" he answered his cell phone sleepily.

"Carter, it's me," Angie cried anxiously into the phone.

"Angie? What time is it? Is something wrong? Are you okay?"

"For now," she answered. "But—"

"What do you mean 'for now'? What's happened?"

"Your grandfather happened."

"What are you talking about?"

"He's got his pal Sheriff Martin believing I set the fire."

"You? But you weren't anywhere near there."

"He doesn't know that," Angie reminded Carter. "No one knows where we were that night."

"Did you tell him?" Suddenly Carter's voice sounded very small and frightened. Angie knew he was afraid that his entire world was crumbling around him.

"Of course not," Angie assured him. "I would never do that to you."

"Oh," he said, sounding relieved. "What did you tell him?"

"Nothing. My lawyer said I didn't have to say anything."

"Your lawyer?"

"The ACLU guy. He's a friend of my aunt's. He helped me out last night because it was an emergency. But, Carter—" Her voice began to break. "He said if this goes any further, I might have to get a criminal attorney. Criminal!"

"It's okay, Angie, please don't cry," Carter begged her. "I'll take care of this. You'll be okay."

"Carter, you can't tell your grandfather about us. Especially after what I said to him tonight. He'll cut you off without a dime, you know that. And then all your dreams . . . You'll never get out of here. You'll be in his web forever." Suddenly the image of Carter's browbeaten father flashed through her mind. "You can't do that. I won't let you."

"What about *your* dreams? Don't they count for anything? My grandfather would ruin your life and never think twice about it. I can't allow you to get in trouble for something you didn't do."

"Carter—"

"Angie, let me handle this." His voice was firm. "Now, you try and get some sleep. It's going to be okay. You'll see."

19

Carter stood outside the Morgan Mills building and stared at the light coming from the large office at the top of the building. His grandfather was already in there. The old man always got to work before anyone else, just so he could see how many of his employees were stumbling in late.

This was his moment of truth. Carter knew the minute he told his grandfather where he and Angie had been the night of the fire, his whole life would change. Probably forever. Carter Morgan, Sr. was a vicious man, capable of just about anything when he was crossed. Carter knew he'd probably be getting off easy if all his grandfather did was cut him off financially.

But there was no way Carter was going to let Angie get in trouble to save his skin. He owed her more than that. Before her he'd been nothing, just another cog in his grandfather's tightly spinning wheel. She'd shown him a whole other side of life—one filled with possibility and passion. She'd saved him. Slowly, Carter walked into the lobby.

"Good morning, Mr. Morgan." The guard at the front desk greeted him in the exact same way he welcomed Carter's grandfather and his father every morning. The sound of it made him feel slightly ill.

"I'm just going up to see my grandfather," Carter explained.

"Okay, but I think there's already someone in there with him," the guard answered. "He went up about a half hour ago with some young man."

"That's all right. I'll just wait in his reception area," Carter told him. He pushed the elevator button and waited. Finally the elevator door opened. Much to Carter's surprise, Ted walked out into the lobby. "What're you doing here?" Carter asked him, confused.

"Oh, hey, C. M.," Ted replied nervously. "I haven't seen you in a while. How was Aspen?"

"Fine. You didn't answer my question."

"Oh, I was just . . . um . . . I was just dropping something off for my dad. He and your grandfather have some sort of deal brewing, I think." He stopped for a moment and breathed easier, knowing he'd come up with a plausible excuse. "How come you're here so early?"

"I'm about to enter my own funeral," Carter groaned.

"Huh?"

"I'm about to piss off my grandfather in a big way."

"How big?"

"Mega-huge. You remember that girl Angie?"

"The skater chick?"

"She's a lot more than a . . ." Carter stopped. What was the use? It wasn't like Ted was going to see Angie for who she really was. "Anyway, for some reason my grandfather's convinced she started the fire at the vacant lot."

Ted smiled slightly. "And you're not?"

"She didn't do it," Carter said firmly. "I know for certain."

"Come on. How do you know that?"

"Because I was with her that night. *All night*. And now I have to tell my grandfather. Considering he forbade me to see her, I'd say my days as the heir of the Morgan fortune are numbered."

"Then don't tell him," Ted advised with a shrug.

"I *have* to tell him," Carter insisted. "He's got the sheriff bothering Angie now."

"Carter, you gotta think about what you're saying here. Is this skater chick . . ."

"Angie."

"Is this *Angie*," Ted repeated, "really worth giving up everything—your family, your friends, your *life*? I mean, come on. How long do you think this thing with her is going to last?"

Carter thought of the promise ring. *Yesterday, today, tomorrow.* "You don't get it, Ted." Carter headed toward the elevator.

But Ted steered him away before he could step in. "Look, you don't have to do this right now. It can wait until the afternoon. Let's walk to school and talk about it. We're probably late already. What time is it?"

Carter looked at the clear plastic watch on his wrist. "Almost eight."

"What happened to your gold Rolex?" Ted asked him.

"I lost it at the cabin the night I was snowed in with Angie. The clasp must have broken while I was shoveling the drive."

"Or that's what she wanted you to believe," Ted remarked casually, seeing a perfect opportunity to finish the job he'd started.

"Who? Angie?"

Ted shrugged. "It was probably the most gold she'd ever seen in one place before. You couldn't really blame her."

"She would never take it. She wouldn't have to. She knows if she wanted it, all she had to do was ask."

"Boy, she's really playing you," Ted said with mock sympathy. "I hope she was worth it. A gold watch is a high price to pay for a night in the sack."

"Ted, man, don't make me hurt you," Carter warned menacingly.

"Think about it, C. M.," Ted continued. "A girl like her, she's probably never been to a place with cloth napkins in her whole life. But you take her all over the place in your fancy car. It had to be a kick for her."

"Don't be ridiculous," Carter snapped back. "Angie's not like that."

"How much do you really know about her? She probably figured giving you a tumble was worth all the free food. It's no big deal to her, she's probably slept with half of Torren."

"Not Angie . . ."

"I just hope you played it safe, man. A girl like that could give a guy some pretty nasty diseases."

285

Carter's mind was racing now. Angie *had* had that condom in her purse, like she was ready for something. *Planning it.* She'd sworn she'd never slept with anyone else, but why would she be carrying a condom if . . . *no!* Ted wasn't right. He *couldn't* be right. He hadn't been there. He didn't know anything about her.

But there were also things Carter didn't know about Angie. And apparently, Ted was more than willing to fill him in on the details. "Did she tell you that she visited that Buzz dude in the hospital the day after the fire?" Ted questioned him. "Jackson's dad's a doctor there. He saw her in the hallway with that wacky aunt of hers."

"Angie visited *Buzz*?" Carter's voice was shaking.

Ted smiled victoriously. He knew he'd found Carter's Achilles' heel. He was obviously jealous of that skater jerk.

Carter's mind was racing now. He'd never really been sure just how Angie felt about him. The jealousy was still there, despite all her protestations that there was nothing between her and Buzz, and never had been.

Ted nodded. "Think about it, C. M. You have to admit she sure stood up for him at that town meeting yesterday. Telling your grandfather he should be concerned about him. She sure seemed concerned. Those two must be pretty hot and heavy for her to have a fit like that in front of everyone."

Carter felt as though someone had kicked him in the stomach. *Angie and Buzz.* It made sense in a horrible way. His mind raced back to that hickey he'd seen on Angie's neck, and the way she'd made him drop her off near Hamburger Heaven after that afternoon in New Charity. Could she have been heading off for some sort of rendezvous with the skater?

"They probably got a big laugh off of you," Ted continued, going in for the kill. "Not to mention all the skateboards a watch like your gold Rolex could buy them. You better check the pawn shops, man. I'm sure you'll find it there."

Carter felt dizzy, like he couldn't breathe. He thought he had put the watch on that morning. But now he wasn't so sure.

"You okay, C. M.?"

"Not right now," he admitted as he turned to leave the building. "But I will be. Come on. We better get to school."

Angie sat by the window at Sk8 4Ever on Monday afternoon, waiting for Carter's convertible to pull into the parking lot. They always met there on Mondays for a skateboarding lesson when the weather permitted. On a drizzly, cold day like today, Carter would probably hang out in the back, keeping Angie company while she painted.

But here it was, six thirty already, and Carter hadn't shown up.

"Hey, Angie, go ahead home," Cody said finally. "There's no one else coming here tonight. Besides, I'm going to close early. I have plans."

"I can close up," Angie told him. "Go ahead, get ready."

"Angie, he's not coming today," Cody said quietly. "It's probably nothing. He just got held up or something."

Angie shook her head. "He would've called. Something happened, I know it."

"Why don't you call him, then?"

"I've been trying. He's not picking up his cell."

Just then the phone in the back office rang. Angie leaped up from her perch by the window and raced for the phone. "I'll get it!" she squealed with relief.

But the voice on the other end of the phone wasn't Carter's. "May I speak to Angie Simms?" a woman asked.

"This is Angie."

"My name is Carolyn Saltz. I'm a reporter for the *Western Pennsylvania Gazette*. I'd like to ask you a few questions about the fire at Morgan Mills."

"How did you get my name?" Angie asked her nervously.

"From the police blotter," the reporter replied. "It's a matter of public record that you've been interrogated. Now, do you know whether or not the police consider you a suspect in this case?"

"Damn it!" Angie shouted in frustration as she slammed down the receiver rather than answer the woman's question.

"What is it?" Cody came racing in.

"That was a reporter for some newspaper. She wanted to know if I thought I was a suspect in the Morgan Mills fire."

"It had to be the old man. He probably had someone tip her off," Cody deduced.

"Why would he do that? I didn't start that fire." She sighed heavily. It was obvious the truth didn't matter anymore. "But by the time he gets finished with me, everyone will think I did."

20

It was nearly three months before Angie saw Carter again. He was standing in the parking lot outside a mall, surrounded by a crowd of his preppie hangers-on. He looked like one of them now, dressed in his school uniform, with his perfectly pleated pants and brown loafers. Even from a distance, Angie could see his new gold watch, bigger and brighter than his old one. It was shimmering in the spring sunlight. *Probably a gift from a grateful grandfather.* His wild bangs, the ones Angie had once so lovingly brushed away from his eyes, were gone now. They were cut short and blended in with the rest of his blond locks. The haircut made him look more like his father than before.

At the moment, he had his arm around a well-dressed, big-breasted, and probably empty-headed blonde, who laughed at his every word and clung to him as though he were a bounty she'd worked hard to catch and would never release.

Angie knew he saw her too. She felt his eyes on her, burning through her heart like fire. And even though there were several feet between them, she could sense his shame when their eyes met.

Good. He should feel shame. He should feel awful for all he'd put me through. There hadn't been any big good-bye scenes, no awful fights or vicious words. Instead there'd been a deafening silence, in the form of a flurry of unreturned phone calls. He hadn't even bothered to give her the decency of a reason. *He'd taken the coward's way out.* She looked down at her empty finger, where her promise ring once sat, and sighed. *Yesterday, today, tomorrow, my ass,* she thought bitterly.

Not that he had to actually tell her his reasons for ending things. Angie knew what had happened. Simply put, Carter wasn't the strong, brave person she'd believed him to be. He was a wimp, just like his father. And in the end, it had been easier for him to give in to his grandfather's wishes—no, make that *demands*—and traded her in for his life of privilege. She didn't have to be psychic like Aunt Dodo to figure that one out.

For a while she'd thought about getting back at him, of telling the police where she'd really been that night, but she knew no one would believe her anyway. Somehow Carter's family would put a sick spin on her story, painting her as a vengeful girl who was lying to get herself out of trouble. The newspapers would have had a field day with that one. And the truth was, she would never do that to Carter. Despite it all, she knew that somewhere, deep down, he was the man she'd once thought he was. Only now, all the humanity in him was so far buried he might never find it again.

The newspapers. For months now, the police had leaked all kinds of lies and suspicions to the press, all leading subtly to Angie, although they admitted they had no actual proof that she'd started the fire. In fact, whoever had committed the arson had been quite good at it, leaving no clues at all. Still, the innuendo that it could have been Angie was enough to make her a pariah in Torren. Hell, her own father could barely look at her anymore, especially after someone else at the mill got the promotion he'd been eyeing. The other skaters weren't much better. Rather than thank Angie for standing up for their rights at the town hall meeting, they'd turned on her completely. She'd heard that Buzz was telling people she was the one who'd started the fire—as revenge for his breaking up with her. That was pretty ironic, considering she was the one who'd broken up with *him*. But, like everything else in this mess, the fiction was a hell of a lot more interesting than the truth. And that was what people chose to believe.

Of course, not everyone thought Angie was guilty. Dodo and Cody knew the truth and had been loyal to her, as had her aunt's friend Michael, who continued to give her legal advice from time to time.

Luckily, Angie knew this hell wasn't going to last forever. Another month and she'd be out of Torren and on her way to Philadelphia. She'd received the acceptance packet from the Philadelphia Art Institute just two weeks ago. She'd known before she'd even opened it that she'd been accepted. The envelope was thickly padded with lots of paper. That's what acceptances looked like. Rejections were nothing more than a slip of paper. Of course, at the time, the acceptance had been bittersweet, since Angie had no real way to pay for school.

And then, out of nowhere, her aunt Dodo had given her the greatest gift Angie could ever receive—enough money to pay for the first semester of art school. After that, Angie could declare herself independent of her family and be eligible for her own financial aid, without any forms from her parents. She'd probably be paying back student loans for years, but it would be worth it.

Angie didn't know for sure how Aunt Dodo had gathered the money for such an expensive gift, but she had noticed that her grandmother's antique silver candlesticks—the only things Dodo had kept of her mother's belongings—were gone from her apartment. When Angie had questioned her aunt, however, she hadn't gotten a straight answer. "Wouldn't that have been a kick?" Dodo'd replied at the time. "Imagine my mother paying for you to get out of Torren. A delicious irony, don't you think?"

In fact, that was why Angie was at the mall that afternoon. She was picking up some of the things she would need for her dorm room. She hadn't expected to see Carter. And she never could have predicted how painful it would be to see him again. She thought she'd gotten past all that. But she hadn't. She wondered if she ever would.

Angie was standing there, staring at Carter,

lost in thought, when her cell phone rang.

"Hello, Angie?" It was Aunt Dodo, her savior, on the line.

"Hi."

"Did you get everything?"

"I got more than I came for," she said ruefully, staring at Carter.

"What's wrong?"

"It's nothing," she replied. "Nothing that matters, anyway. What's up?"

"A letter came for you from the college. I think it might be your schedule. You want me to bring it over to Sk8 4Ever for you? Or should I just leave it in your room?"

Her schedule. That made it real. She was actually getting out of Torren and starting her life as an artist.

"Could you bring it over?" she practically squealed with excitement into the phone. "I'll be there in ten minutes."

She clicked off the phone and raced out of the parking lot, leaving Carter and the rest of those preppie creeps behind.

"Let me see it!" Angie shouted excitedly as she raced into Sk8 4Ever. She ran past Cody to get to Aunt Dodo.

"Hi there," Cody teased her. "Remember me? Your boss? The one who pays you every week?"

"Hi Cody," Angie said, laughing.

Cody smiled at her. It had been a long time since he'd heard her hearty chuckle.

"Here you go," Dodo said, handing her the slim white envelope. "I hope you got into that sketch class you wanted."

"I don't know, Aunt Dodo, that's really for sophomores and I—oh no!" Her face fell as she scanned the letter.

"It's okay, Angie," Dodo said. "You can get the class you wanted next semester."

Angie shook her head. "There isn't going to be any second semester. There isn't going to be anything." She handed Dodo the note from the school.

Dear Ms. Simms,

It has come to our attention that you have been the subject of a criminal investigation in the Township of Torren, PA. While we support the belief that you are innocent until proven guilty, we are concerned about your ability to complete your studies to the best of your ability during this difficult time. It is for that reason that we regretfully must rescind our acceptance of you as a student at our school, at least for the time being. Of course, we will reconsider your application when the investigation into this crime has been completed.

Sincerely,
The Office of the Registrar

Dodo's eyes were blazing as she read the note. She looked up at Cody. "This has gone on long enough!" she exclaimed with a vehemence Angie had never seen in her before. "Carter is going to have to go to the police and tell the truth."

"He's never going to do that," Angie moaned. "He'll never stand up to his grandfather. He's too afraid of what will happen if he does."

"Well then, someone is going to have to convince him that you can survive without being an heir to the Morgan fortune." Dodo stared pointedly at Cody.

Cody was quiet. "Why are you looking at *me*?" he asked finally.

"Because you're the one who's going to have to do the convincing," Dodo told him in no uncertain terms.

"And why would Carter Morgan III ever listen to me?" Cody said, trying to change the subject.

"Because," Dodo pressed. "No one knows better than *you* what it feels like to be shunned by Carter Morgan, Sr.," she told him firmly.

Cody lowered his eyes and fell silent. "I don't know what you're talking about, Dorothy," he finally said.

"Neither do I, Aunt Dodo," Angie insisted. "Why would Cody know anything about Carter's grandfather?"

"Not *Cody*," Dodo corrected her. "Angie, allow me to introduce you to Edward Morgan, the younger, rebellious son of Carter Morgan, Sr."

Angie stared at her aunt. Had she gone crazy? "Cody? Come on, Aunt Dodo. That's impossible."

"Not at all," Dodo corrected her. "Tell her, *Edward.*"

Cody didn't say a word.

"If that's true, then why didn't Carter say anything to me about Cody being his uncle?"

"Because he doesn't know about me," Cody

admitted quietly. "Once my father decides you aren't part of the fold, you cease to exist. Carter's father, my brother, was forbidden to ever mention me to him. Or to anyone." He turned to Dodo. "How long have you known?"

"I've always known," she told him softly. "I was just waiting for you to admit it."

"But how?"

Dodo laughed. "You can fool a lot of people with that big beard, and about forty extra pounds. And I have to admit that the plastic surgery you've had because of your accident has changed the entire shape of your face. But I'd recognize those eyes anywhere. They haven't changed very much—other than to add a little more sadness and experience. I've known who you are all along. And I suspect your father has too."

"You recognized my eyes?" Cody sounded confused. "But that's impossible. I never knew you before I met Angie."

"No," Dodo agreed. "But I knew who you were. I've been in love with you since, well, since I can remember."

"What are you talking about?" Cody asked her.

"You were once a legend in this town, Edward," Dodo reminded him. She turned to Angie. "You should have seen him. He was such a rebel. He had this thick, dark hair and this really long, lean body. He drove his father crazy with his skateboarding and running away to the ocean so he could surf during the summer. Everyone knew about him. Most of the preppie kids stayed away from him because even though he was rich, he was so different than they were. And my friends, well . . . we would never even dare approach a Morgan. But I knew who you were, Edward. I watched you."

"All those years, and you never once said anything to him?" Angie asked.

"Not a peep. I was a lot shyer in those days. And I was definitely more class-conscious. It wasn't until I went to Europe that I realized that money doesn't make you superior to anyone."

Angie thought for a moment. Dodo had returned to Torren about five years ago. That was just after Cody had appeared on the scene. "Aunt Dodo, the unfinished business you came back for—that was Cody, wasn't it?"

Dodo nodded. "I'd been following Edward's career for years, and I'd heard about the accident. Then one day your mother wrote me and told me about some surfing and skateboarding stranger who'd moved to Torren and opened a skateboard shop. I just put two and two together."

She paused for a moment, thinking. "There's just one thing I've never figured out. Why did you come back *here* to open the shop? Why would you ever want to be this close to your father?"

"It's *all* about my father," Cody explained. "Talk about unfinished business. In his eyes, I've always been a loser. He had no respect for what I'd accomplished. And then the accident happened. For a while I sort of wandered around feeling sorry for myself. I actually started believing that my father had been right about me."

Dodo moved closer to him and linked her arm through his. "He was *never* right about you," she assured him.

Cody nodded. "I know that now, but it sure took a lot of time and self-pity before I could figure it out. I eventually realized that everything in life has a purpose, and that my accident was a sign. It was time for me to do something for other people, instead of just trying to win a bunch of trophies. So I decided to build a skatepark where skaters could do their thing safely. That way, what happened to me didn't have to happen to anyone else. Unfortunately, I didn't get the money together in time to help Buzz."

"But why *here*?" Dodo asked again.

"I guess I wanted to be sure my father would

be aware that I was doing something good."
Cody shrugged. "But of course he killed that
when he bought the land out from under me.
There's not going to be any skatepark in Torren."

"I don't know about that," Dodo murmured quietly.

"What?" Cody asked her.

"Never mind. It's just a feeling," Dodo told
him. "Anyway, the thing is, you don't need to
build a skatepark to make a difference. You can
make a difference in people's lives on a much
smaller scale and it still will mean a lot. If you
do the right thing, I guarantee your father will
find out about it. I don't know if *he'll* be pleased
or proud of you, but I'm sure I will be."

The next afternoon, Carter left his prep school
planning to meet Ted and a few of the others for
pizza. But before he could meet up with them,
a familiar face stopped him on the street.
"Cody," Carter said with surprise. "What are
you doing here?"

"Actually, my name's Edward Morgan," his
uncle told him. "And there's something I need
to talk to you about."

21

The next morning, Angie was woken up by a loud banging on her door. "Angie, wake up," Dodo exclaimed excitedly. "You're not going to believe this!"

Angie sat up with a start. She leaped out of bed, rubbed the sleep from her eyes, and opened the door. Dodo practically threw the morning paper at her. "Read it!" she insisted as she burst into Angie's bedroom.

Angie unfolded the paper and stared at the headline: MORGAN GRANDSON CLEARS SIMMS GIRL.

She studied the paper for a moment, unable to believe her eyes. "He did it," she murmured quietly. "He stood up to the old sonuvabitch."

"Yeah, he did," Dodo agreed. "In the end,

Carter turned out to be a stand-up guy."

"In the end," Angie repeated bitterly. "It took him long enough. It's been four months since that fire."

"He was up against a lot, Angie," Dodo said softly.

"So was I," Angie reminded her. "I was the one plastered all over the papers, remember?"

"But you were raised to be strong. You've always been able to take care of yourself. Carter . . . well . . . sometimes it's not such a great thing to be given everything. You're never really sure if you're going to be able to stand on your own two feet."

Angie paused for a moment, considering what her aunt had just said. She knew it was the truth. "He must be petrified right now."

"I would guess so," Dodo agreed. "But he's got Edward. He's been through this. He'll help him along."

Edward. Angie wondered if she'd ever get used to calling Cody by his given name. The thought was interrupted by her cell phone ringing. She ignored it completely.

"Aren't you going to answer that?" Dodo asked her.

"Nah. It's probably just some stupid reporter

wanting a comment. I don't ever want to talk to one of them again."

"I really think you should answer it," Dodo urged.

There was something in her aunt's tone that convinced Angie to do as she said. She picked up the phone and clicked the answer button. "Hello?"

"Angie."

Hearing his voice again was a shock. "Carter."

"Angie, I'm so sorry."

He was crying now, she could tell. But her heart had hardened a lot in the past few months. Betrayal could do that to a person. "You should be."

"I know I should have told them right away," Carter continued, begging her forgiveness. "I tried to. But Ted was so sure that you . . . and then my entire family . . . oh, never mind. It doesn't matter anymore."

"No, I guess it doesn't," Angie agreed.

"I've already made sure that the sheriff's department faxed a copy of my statement to your school, along with a letter saying that you weren't a suspect in the case. They'll reinstate your acceptance, I know it."

"Thanks," Angie said. "I'm sure they will."

"Angie, please, you sound so far away. I need to see you. I want to explain."

"There's no explanation necessary, Carter," she assured him. "I'm grateful for what you've done. I know what it's cost you."

"Telling the truth didn't cost me as much as *not* telling did," he said, his voice aching with longing for her. He paused for a moment, gathering the courage he needed. "I know I have no right to ask you this, but I *have* to. Cody—I mean, my uncle Edward—says he thinks you and I still have a chance. And I believe him. Can't we at least talk? We meant so much to each other once. That has to count for something."

"You're right," she said slowly.

"Then you'll meet me?" he asked hopefully.

"No. I'm just agreeing with you. You have no right to ask me that." She hung up the phone and began to cry bitterly. Whoever said closure was a good thing was a moron.

From the moment Angie's name was cleared, the town of Torren was turned upside down. The police had no suspects in the fire, and for a few weeks it looked as though whoever had commited the arson was going to get away with it.

Then Ted Parker was stopped for speeding and driving under the influence. When the police searched his car, they found traces of kerosene, and a high-powered lighter. The kerosene matched the fuel that had been used to start the fire at the vacant lot beside the mill.

Ted, of course, swore up and down that the fire hadn't been his idea. He told the police that it was all part of Carter Morgan, Sr.'s plan to get rid of the skaters once and for all. He'd just been doing the old man's bidding.

There was no telling whether or not the police believed Ted. It didn't matter, anyhow. They'd never actually press charges against Carter Morgan, Sr. Hell, he had half the judges in the county in his back pocket, not to mention the district attorney and the sheriff. Ted Parker was going down alone.

At least *legally*. Surprisingly, one of the few people to believe Ted Parker was Lila Morgan— Carter Morgan, Sr.'s wife. She knew better than anyone just how ruthless her husband could be. There was no doubt in her mind that he had done exactly what Ted had accused him of.

Which was probably why she insisted that

Carter Morgan, Sr. turn the deed to the vacant lot over to his younger son, Edward. Nobody knew just what she'd threatened her husband with, but it turned out that Torren would have its skatepark after all.

In the weeks before she left for school, Angie had spent a lot of time designing a logo for the park. She'd eventually come up with an abstract airbrushed image of a skater with his board. It hadn't been easy getting it approved by the skatepark's assistant manager, Buzz McGrath. As it turned out, he had a real eye for detail. He instinctively knew what image it would take to market the skatepark to both professionals and novices. And Buzz was really going after the professionals in a big way. He'd already booked some minor comps at the park, and he was looking to attract bigger ones in the future. What a shock to find out Buzz had a head for business. He would be a real asset to the skatepark, and to Torren. How was that for a switch?

Angie wasn't there to see her logo painting appear on the park's opening day. By the time construction began on the Morgan Skateboard Arena, she was long gone.

Epilogue

The cold November air blew hard as Angie and her friends wandered into the coffee bar in West Philadelphia. They'd spent the day sketching the architectural features of some of the old houses around the University of Pennsylvania. Their charcoal-stained fingers were cold, their throats were parched, and nothing would make them happier than a hot espresso.

"So you're not going home for Thanksgiving?" Rhiannon, a small blonde with a penchant for purple, asked Angie as she sat down in one of the coffee bar's comfortable easy chairs.

"Nope," Angie said. "It would take a lot more than a turkey to get me back to Torren."

"But isn't your aunt going to miss you?" Angie's friend Maddy asked as she took off her black beret and smoothed her ponytail.

"I doubt it. She and her boyfriend Cody . . . I mean Edward . . . are going to Paris for a long weekend."

"A weekend in Paris," Rhiannon mused. "That sounds so romantic."

"I guess so," Angie shrugged. She plopped down onto one of the couches.

"Forget romance. At this point, I'd just take a hug," Maddy joked. "It's been a long time since I've had any real male companionship . . . if you know what I mean. I swear there are no good men left in this whole city."

"Oh, I wouldn't say that," Rhiannon joked. "Check out the guy behind the counter."

"Mmm . . . tasty," Maddy agreed. "I wouldn't kick him out of my bed."

Angie giggled and turned around to get a good look at the object of her friends' fantasies. "Oh my God," she blurted out suddenly. *"Carter."*

The girls stared at her.

"You know him?" Maddy asked. "And you haven't brought him around? A stud like that? You've been holding out on us, girl."

"I didn't know he was here," she said quietly. "I thought I'd left him behind me."

But she hadn't. And as he turned slightly, wiping the long bangs from his eyes and revealing a small hoop in his left ear, she knew he hadn't forgotten her either. "Excuse me," she told her friends in a small, shaky voice.

He saw her coming right away. Their eyes locked, and Angie felt a familiar tingle go through her body. She stood there for a moment, staring at him, trying to discern whether this was really happening to her or if it was all a dream.

"Angie," he said, taking her hand in his. "I knew we would meet up. Your aunt swore to me that we would."

"I didn't know you were in Philadelphia," Angie remarked slowly. "I can't believe it."

"I tried to get your address or phone number from Dodo and Edward, but they wouldn't give it to me. They weren't sure you'd want them to."

Angie nodded. They were probably right.

"Dodo said if it was meant to be, we'd find each other. I've never stopped thinking of you. Angie, you and I . . ."

"That was a long time ago, Carter." *A lifetime ago.*

He turned to his coworker, a short girl

with an eager grin and huge teeth. "Hey Shelli, can you handle things for a few minutes?"

Shelli nodded. "No problem. Sammy's on his way back any second now anyway."

"Thanks." Carter walked out from behind the coffee bar and took Angie by the hand, leading her to a secluded table near the back. His touch sent a fresh spurt of electricity through her, and though she'd tried to hide the excitement, she could tell he'd noticed. She'd never been able to keep anything from him.

"What are you doing here?" she asked him.

"You mean in Philadelphia?"

"I mean working in a coffee bar," Angie said, indicating the blue-and-red apron he was wearing.

"I've got to find some way to pay for the University of Pennsylvania," Carter said. "I've got a bunch of student loans, but they don't cover books and meals. So I'm working here."

So the old man really had cut him off. Angie smiled warmly at him. "You've always been willing to work for the things you really want."

He looked searchingly into her deep green eyes. "I'll do anything," he told her, making sure she understood the meaning behind his words.

Angie fought to move her gaze from his.

He'd hurt her so badly. She didn't want to fall back into that trap again. "Um, so, uh, what are you studying?" she asked, struggling to make idle conversation. *To keep things light and safe.*

"Well, I'm a poly-sci major right now, but I want to go to law school. I'm thinking of going into labor relations. I could make a difference helping unions get better wages and safer conditions in factories. After all, I have inside knowledge of just how much mangement is really able to provide—if they're pushed hard enough."

"Labor relations, huh? Boy, that'd really piss off your grandfather," she joked.

"Whatever." Carter dismissed the idea. "I'm not doing it to piss him off. I don't care what he thinks of me, good or bad. I've spent too long worrying about him. And it's cost me more dearly than you'll ever know."

Angie looked at him. She could tell he was telling her the truth. Except he was wrong. She knew how much it had cost him. *How much it had cost us both.*

"Hey Angie, we're heading back to Center City. You coming?" Rhiannon called to her.

"Just one minute," she replied. She turned back to Carter. "I guess I should go."

Carter took her hand and held it tight. It was as though he was afraid that if he let her leave again, she would be gone forever. "Angie, please," he pleaded.

"Carter, I'm afraid. So afraid," she told him honestly.

"I don't blame you. But Angie, I promise you . . ."

"You promised me before, Carter," she reminded him. Her tone was gentle, without even a trace of anger.

"That was before. I made a huge mistake. I trusted the wrong people when I should have believed in you. I know that now. I don't blame you for doubting me. But so much has changed. Can't you see that?"

She studied him for a moment, searching his face for a sign. She found it in his eyes. They were different somehow, dotted with wild specks of freedom and a sense of personal confidence that hadn't been there before. Carter was his own person now. He was a new man.

Despite her misgivings, this new man was someone Angie was very much interested in getting to know. "We could talk or something," she said finally, pulling out her sketch pad and scribbling her local cell phone number on a piece of paper. She slid it to him across the table.

"*Angie,*" Maddy urged. "We've gotta go."

Carter smiled up at her. "I'll call you."

"I know you will. But Carter, we've got to take it easy," she warned him. "I'm not going to rush into anything. This time I need to be sure. I can't go through that again."

"I know, Angie. I would never pressure you into something you didn't want. I'll take it slow, just like you want."

She was barely three blocks from the coffee shop when her cell phone began to ring. She laughed heartily and took it from her purse. "Hello, Carter," she said into the receiver. "What took you so long?"